THE WILD MAGIC TRILOGY

BOOK 3

The Promise Witch

CELINE KIERNAN

WALKER BOOKS

First published 2020 by Walker Books Ltd
87 Vauxhall Walk, London SE11 5HJ

2 4 6 8 10 9 7 5 3 1

Text © 2020 Celine Kiernan
Cover art and interior illustrations © 2019, 2020 Jessica Courtney-Tickle

The right of Celine Kiernan to be identified as author of this
work has been asserted by her in accordance with the
Copyright, Designs and Patents Act 1988

This book has been typeset in Joanna

Printed and bound by CPI Group (UK) Ltd, Croydon CR0 4YY

British Library Cataloguing in Publication Data:
a catalogue record for this book is available from the British Library

ISBN 978-1-4063-7393-6

www.walker.co.uk

To those brave souls who stand up to cruelty. Thank you.

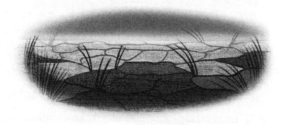

The Parched World

Still in her pyjamas, Mup climbed out of her bedroom window and into the shimmering heat. It was early morning, the palace peaceful with sleep, but already the air felt too hot to breathe.

It's only May, Mup thought. *What will it be like when summer really starts?*

The sky was a heartless scald of blue overhead, the narrow granite windowsill roasting beneath her feet. Mup curled her toes around the edge and looked down. The walls of the castle plummeted sharply away beneath her. Far below, the courtyard wavered in a mirage-dance of heat.

I'm like a small bird, she thought, *standing on the edge of a cliff.*

Mup took a breath, closed her eyes and let herself topple. She fell down and down. The air sped past, ruffling her colourful pyjamas and streaming her twists of hair back like dark snakes. *Lovely*, she thought, spreading her arms. *Lovely and cool.*

She opened her eyes. The ground was rushing towards her. Every flagstone, every war-cracked seam in the cobbles zoomed close. Mup arched her back, turned her face to the sky, and swooped a swallow-graceful arc up, away from the looming ground, through the oven-heat of the enclosing walls and into clear morning air above the castle.

A hot breeze blew up there, so horribly dry that Mup felt it suck the moisture from her skin.

On the battlements to her right, sentries ran forward. Men and women alike, they shaded their eyes against the sunshine, and gazed anxiously up to where Mup floated high in the buffeting air.

They were worried for her safety.

Mup gave them a little wave: *I'm OK.*

She pointed that they go back into the shade. Instead, they launched themselves into their raven forms and rose upwards in a cawing flock. For a moment the beating of many dark wings disturbed the air around Mup. Then the ravens were above her, climbing the hot air draughts on outspread wings, wheeling far overhead, patrolling the skies for threat.

Sighing, Mup turned her attention to the castle and

surrounding forest below. She took it all in – the square, stone severity of the buildings, the brittle fragility of the trees – and she felt at once hopeful and sad. It was all so beautiful. It was all balanced so delicately on the edge of ruin.

Like an egg on a tightrope, as Dad would say.

Slowly, watching all around her, Mup floated out across the top of the river wall and down to the heat-cracked riverbed. The woods surrounding the castle should have been fresh and green at this time of year, but the heat had crisped them to a parched brown. Leaves fell in unseasonable drifts to the shimmering earth.

Mup's feet sent up a puff of dust as she landed in the centre of what had been the castle river. Once, little fish had peeped and played where she now stood. Once, crayfish and snails had led their slow, creeping lives. It had been cool and safe for them. A green world of waving river weed. Now there was nothing but dust and the sad whisper of dead leaves falling from the dying forest.

Everything had been going so well till now.

By working hard and pulling together, the people of Witches Borough had survived the terrible curse-winter that Mup's grandmother had sent to break them. Village had helped clan, clan had helped river-folk, and the castle had become the place where everyone met to plan and coordinate. A real, proper sense of community had grown as people joined together to help each other survive the interminable snow.

Then the snow had disappeared. As quickly as it had arrived, it simply melted away. Spring opened its bright green leaves to the sky, and everyone thought they'd won.

"The old queen has admitted defeat," they cheered. "She will leave us alone!"

Witches Borough could finally get on with building a new life.

About one month later, the castle inhabitants awoke to find the river gone.

Mup remembered the morning well. They had rushed down to find fishes flopping and gasping in the slippery weed, frogs and newts stunned, the riverbanks already drying.

The next day the heat came, the clouds disappeared, and the thirsty time began.

That had been a month ago. It had not rained in Witches Borough since.

First, Grandma tried to freeze us out, thought Mup, kneeling down into the dust of the parched riverbed. *Now she's trying to thirst us.*

She lay on her stomach, and pressed her ear to the hot ground.

Hello, she thought. *Can you hear me?*

Far, far beneath her, there answered a tiny, thready, muffled voice. The sound of the river, sucked below and desperate; trapped underground by the terrible, invincible, bitter power of Mup's grandmother. Mup spread her hands, pressed her palms to the earth. She was the pathfinder, after all. She was the stitcher of worlds. Surely she could find a path to the water? Surely she could lead the water home?

She closed her eyes and concentrated.

We're looking for you, she thought. *You're not alone down there. We'll find you.*

There came no reply. Mup could still sense the river down there, shifting and lost, as if wandering some subterranean labyrinth just out of her reach. Above and around it, the earth ached; so sad and thirsty that even touching it made Mup want to cry.

A shadow fell across the parched ground. Mup looked up to see her mother floating down from the top of the boat steps. Her dark hair and dark silk dressing gown fluttered in the hot air. Her pale face was grim as she surveyed their surroundings.

"You shouldn't keep coming out here alone, Mup."

"The land is getting sicker, Mam."

Mam landed lightly by her side, crouched, and pressed her fingers to the earth next to Mup's splayed hand. She grimaced in sympathetic pain. She glared out at the hot wind, the angry sun, the blank and gleeful sky. She whispered to the bitter old woman who was controlling them all. "I'm telling you now, Mother. You will not win."

Mup nodded in fierce agreement. *We'll stop her.*

But how?

There came a flash of shadows as the sentries swooped low, cawing a warning. Mam and Mup shot to their feet. Lightning flashed at their fingertips as they stared towards the bend in the river where the guards' attention was focused. For a moment there was nothing, then a sound became audible there – the sound of people singing.

Mam relaxed. "Choral magic," she whispered.

"Clann'n Cheoil!" cried Mup. "The kids are here!"

A smile softened Mam's expression. "The very first class for our new school."

A little band of children came into view around the bend. There were about twenty of them. Made minuscule by the castle looming to their right and the steep riverbank to their left, they ranged in age from five to maybe twelve. Mup swelled with pride to see them. No matter how closely they huddled together, or how scared they seemed, she was proud of how brave they were for coming here. And she was proud of their parents, who so believed in Mam that they would risk sending their children to her, despite the threat still posed to them by the old queen.

There were no castle children in this group. Unlike Clann'n Cheoil – who had brought their children home as soon as they could – the Speirling and castle staff and other aristocrats of the borough had yet to call their children back from the distant boarding schools where many of them lived.

Maybe castle people don't believe in Mam as much as ordinary people do, Mup thought.

Maybe they still thought Mam was going to lose.

The children advanced through the heat haze, their eyes fixed on the ravens patrolling the skies above. Despite the brutal sunshine, they walked in cool shade, thanks to a hazy parasol of summer cloud that drifted just above their heads. This cloud was being created by the beautiful voices of the men and women who accompanied the children – members of Clann'n Cheoil who had vowed to protect any students on their daily journeys to and from the school. A soft, subtle, silver-and-white confection, the cloud evaporated as quickly as the clann could conjure it. It took all their magical energies to keep singing it into being, and they sang in turns, voices lifting into and dropping from the melody as some of them took up the thread and others paused for a moment to rest.

These adults were familiar to Mup. The Clann'n Cheoil had fought with her mother against the old queen, and had stayed with her through all the perilous months afterwards. They were loyal and independent. None more so than the tall silver-haired woman who led the children through the swirling dust of the river floor: Fírinne, leader of the clann, Mam's loudest supporter and sometimes terrifyingly fierce best friend. Mup waved to her. Fírinne winked.

Mam stepped forward. The children faltered at the sight of her. Mup knew why. Mam was so like a raggedy witch: all pale skin, all black eyes, all dark and flowing hair. Even her dark dressing gown – such a difference to Mam's usual jeans and T-shirts – drifted around her in a manner uncomfortably reminiscent of a raggedy witch's cloak.

It's OK, thought Mup, smiling at the children's hesitant faces. You'll get used to her.

"Mam, I'm going to get Crow, so we can welcome the kids when they come inside."

Mam nodded, and Mup launched herself upwards. The children stepped out from under their cloud, gasping and shouting as Mup shot away from them in a swirl of dust and dead leaves.

I suppose you'll have to get used to me too, she thought as she zoomed like a cloud-shadow up the side of the castle, heading for the chimney smoke which drifted from her best friend's home, high on the battlements above.

In the first few months after he and Dad had fixed up the vardo, Crow had moved around quite a bit, "looking for a decent campsite". Finally he had settled on this spot, high on a patch of flat roof, facing the forest where *Clann'n Cheoil* camped, and looking down onto the wide cool expanse of the castle river.

Back when there was a river, thought Mup.

She rose to the level of Crow's campsite, and his beautiful little home came into view. The vardo nestled in a small garden of potted plants, which Crow kept carefully watered from the castle's last remaining well. *Who'd have thought Crow would turn out to be a farmer?* thought Mup, smiling at the lush herbs, the bee-visited early flowers, the potted apple trees and vegetables. The rooftop garden was quiet; the vardo's painted shutters firmly closed, the door shut tight.

Hovering at the edge of the roof, Mup cawed the special polite call that Crow had taught her – the one which meant, "I'm here. Is it OK if I come closer?"

Crow had explained that this was like knocking on someone's door before walking into their room, or ringing the doorbell before entering someone's house. "Just because you can walk into my camp, doesn't meant you should," he'd told her, as he and Dad put the finishing touches to his caravan. "The whole camp will be my house, not just the vardo."

Mup had never forgotten that. She'd made mistakes before with Crow, and hurt him by not listening to him. She was determined never to do that again.

She floated patiently, waiting for Crow's answering call.

None came.

Maybe her friend wasn't home?

But the smoke rising from the vardo chimney told her otherwise. Crow would never leave a fire burning if he wasn't home. Maybe the breeze had carried her voice away?

Mup tentatively drifted closer, cleared her throat to call again, then paused.

What was that sound?

Somewhere within the closed-up vardo someone

was singing. Faint, dark, very sweet, the song was beautiful in a way that Mup found disturbing. Through the heat and the over-bright sunshine, it seemed to spread a dark web around the brightly coloured wagon. It seemed to hint of shadows, of depths beyond the daylight, of a black river running below the surface of all things. Hypnotic, it drew Mup in, pulling her forward, her discomfort growing even as she bobbed closer.

Before Mup knew it, she found herself right up against the wall of the vardo. How had she got here without noticing? The magic was painfully thick here. The song too loud. Shadows seemed to swarm unseen. The sunlight felt fragile. Yelling in terror, Mup slapped herself away from the painted wood, sending herself spinning back the way she'd come.

The song within the vardo stopped. The dark power fell away.

Crow's voice called uncertainly from within. "Is ... is someone there?"

Mup slammed to a halt against a little raised parapet. Sunshine fell down around her in a shower of heat and light. She clung, gasping, to the stone – not at all certain what had just happened. Behind her, a latch clicked quietly and the door of the vardo creaked open. Crow's tousled head peered around the door frame. His huge dark eyes were wary.

"Mup?" he said. "Have you...?" He looked behind him. He came outside and closed the door. "Have you been there long?" he asked.

"Was that you singing, Crow?"

Crow didn't answer.

"What was that song?" asked Mup.

Crow didn't seem to know what to say for a moment, then he lifted his chin as if in defiance.

"It was just one of Crow's dreaming songs.

I make them up as I go along."

"I'm ... I'm not sure I liked it, Crow."

His eyes widened in offence.

"Why ever not? It's Crow's own song.

If it comes from Crow, can it be wrong?"

Mup didn't know what to say to that.

Crow softened at her obvious discomfort. Obviously in a rhyming mood today, he said:

"Don't worry, girl who is my friend,

I'll fix the music in the end.

I've not yet got the notes quite right,

If I sing them wrong they can cause ... they can cause..."

Mup waited patiently as Crow searched for the best word.

He beamed when he found it: "They can cause fright!"

The two of them grinned at each other across the heat-shimmered air.

"Good rhyme," said Mup. "All your practice is paying off."

Crow puffed his chest.

> *"Never again, in life to come,*
> *Will rhyming steal Crow's words or tongue.*
> *Rhyming is MINE now,*
> *where and when I choose,*
> *to make good songs with*
> *and tell my truths."*

He seemed to be back to his usual brash self, but Mup couldn't help thinking her friend looked a little feverish, his eyes dark-ringed and at the same time over-bright.

"Maybe ... maybe you could talk to Fírinne about that particular song, though, Crow? Get her to teach you how to sing it properly? It feels like very strong magic."

Crow blinked at her.

"Maybe," he said.

Mup nodded awkwardly. It was obvious Crow wasn't keen to pursue this conversation.

She gestured behind her. "The kids are here for the first day at school."

"Already?" Crow shook himself into his raven form.

"Let's go!"

He flapped away over the rooftops.

Mup paused before following him. She looked around at the sun-filled rooftop. Everything seemed fine. Crow's carefully tended pots of herbs and vegetables, the beautifully painted vardo, all were silent, all peaceful, slumbering in the sun. Still, she couldn't help staring at the shadows pooled beneath the wagon; were they a little too thick there? Was the silence a little too … too listening?

Mup shivered. *You're being silly,* she thought. *Crow's magic is rough around the edges. That's all. He's learning, just like the rest of us.*

Still, she kept her eyes on the shadows as she backed away, only turning at the last minute before launching herself after her friend.

She caught up quickly. They flew together between sun-blasted towers, skimmed heat-shimmered ridge tiles, dodged chimneys, until finally they breasted the edged of a parapet, swooped down into an internal courtyard, and landed at the back door of the new school.

Crow looked Mup up and down as he rose into his boy form. For the first time Mup noticed how unusually neat he was, even his tangle of hair seemed somewhat tamed. He made a point of straightening his colourful jacket.

"The question I ask myself, girl-sometimes-hare,

Is shall you be changing from your sleeping-wear?
It seems a tad rude, if not to say crass,
To appear so dishevelled on the first day of class."

Mup looked down at herself. She was still dressed in her pyjamas and her feet were bare.

Every inch of her was covered in dust.

"Oh dear," she sighed. "I got a little distracted this morning."

Crow raised an eyebrow as the sound of voices rose up from within the building.

"Well, it's too late now to make an impression,
You're stuck wearing jammies to this morning's lesson."

And he let himself into the classroom, leaving Mup to dust herself down as best she could.

A Rebel School for Rebel Children

Mup smiled as she stepped into the classroom. She had helped Mam choose this room. Desks and chairs waited patiently for new occupants. Bookcases were ripe with untold adventure. A row of glasses twinkled next to jugs of water, in case the children were thirsty after their long walk to school. Bright, airy windows and a stained-glass door opened onto the courtyard garden from which Mup and Crow had just entered. The children would be able to run around this garden, if they liked, or fly among the trees, or nestle in the mud at the bottom of the tiny pond which, before the drought, had brightened the centre of the lawn.

"Whatever the students need to learn, let them learn it," Mam had told the teachers. "Whatever they need to become, let them become it."

Mup wiggled her toes in one of the bright splashes of

colour which the stained-glass threw across the floor. *It's perfect,* she thought. *They're going to love it.*

On the opposite side of the room a door led to an interior corridor, which led to a flight of steps, which led to the old guardroom, which opened onto the riverside courtyard.

Tipper's voice echoed happily from the shadows there. "This way, childrens! Follow me!"

With a skitter of claws and a merry bark, Mup's little brother bounded into the room. All fat paws, all waving tail, all jolly golden face, he lolloped merrily around the desks, barked "Hello, Crow! Hello, Mup! Hello, hello!" and bounced right back out again.

Grinning, Mup ran after him to wait in the doorway. The new students were edging down the steps and into the corridor. They were a row of owlish faces in the gloom. The light of the riverside courtyard seeped in from the cloakroom behind them. Fírinne was a tall shape within the door there, standing guard. Mup waved up to her. Fírinne raised a hand in reply.

Dad's distinctive, broad-shouldered silhouette joined the tall, slim clann leader. Fírinne leaned on one side of the door frame, her arms crossed, Dad leaned on the other, and the two of them began talking in low voices. Mup knew they were discussing the safety of these children, the possibility of Mup's grandmother engineering some kind of vengeance against their parents.

Crow came to Mup's side, and the approaching children eyed the two of them cautiously.

Mup beamed at them and flung her arms wide. "Welcome to Magic School!"

Unsmiling, the silent children crept past and into the classroom.

"It'll be OK," Mup said gently. "It'll be OK. I promise."

Tipper bounded about, excitedly barking. He snuffled pockets and licked tentatively reaching hands. The children began to smile. They began to look around the sunny room. *Whatever they'd expected,* Mup thought, *it can't have been this bright, happy, noisy place.*

"Fírinne!" barked Tipper, running to the schoolroom door. "Fírinne, where is Badger? You said you'd help him down the stairs!"

Fírinne's voice rose up in the guardroom and all the children laughed as Mup's dear old grey-faced labrador, Badger, floated down the corridor, into the room, and was deposited gently by the door. Delighted with himself, Badger strolled from child to enchanted child, stiffly wagging his tail and introducing himself with polite licks on their outstretched hands.

24

Crow began solemnly handing out copybooks and pens, a name badge for each pupil.

Tipper noticed a tiny girl lurking at the door. "Come in! Come in!" he barked.

The little girl just stared.

Mup went to her. "No need to be scared," she whispered. "No one will hurt you."

The little girl seemed to doubt this. "Not even teacher?" she asked.

At the word "teacher" the other children went silent. They seemed to withdraw.

"Will ... will teacher be here soon?' asked one of the boys.

"Teacher's *already* here," grunted Crow, with his usual lack of tact.

The children gasped. Their eyes darted to the big desk at the front of the room.

The sunlight streaming in the windows there had made it easy to miss the ghost. To a passing glance she could be mistaken for just a shadow. But once you knew she was there, there was no missing her, and once you'd seen her, there was no mistaking the tall, dark-clad spectre for anything other than what she was – a raggedy witch.

With a quiet hiss of fear, the children stepped backwards.

The little girl hid her face in the bright legs of Mup's pyjamas

"It's OK," said Mup. "It's just Naomi. Didn't your parents tell you she'd be here?"

The same Naomi chose that unfortunate moment to drift into shadow. Her severe features leapt into focus, and the children moaned.

Mup made a frustrated gesture at the lurking spirit. *Try not to look so terrifying.* Perhaps it wasn't possible for the ghost to actually change from her terrible uniform, but surely a smile wasn't beyond the realms of her spectral capabilities?

The children began edging for the door.

"Come on, now," urged Mup, desperately trying to prise the little girl from around her waist. "Let's ... let's everyone choose a seat."

"Not a chance," growled one of the older boys. He grabbed his little brother, and ran.

"Wait!" called Crow.

"Wait there, friends.

This witch is here to make amends.

She'll teach us all we wish to know.

In magic skills she'll help us grow!"

His words had no effect.

"Naomi is nice!" cried Mup. "I promise!" But the

children were hurrying away, the older ones dragging smaller ones with them as they went.

A friendly voice, from nowhere and everywhere at once, brought everyone to a halt.

"Hello," it echoed. "Hello! Am I late?"

It was such a warm voice, so full of infectious enthusiasm, that the children crept back to see to whom it belonged. They giggled when the ghost of Doctor Emberly popped his head through the wall at the far end of the room. His head and his ruffled lace collar were all that could be seen. He looked like a great luminous daisy pinned to the bookshelves.

"Oh, I am late!" he cried, taking in the semi-deserted room.

Bustling his way through the blackboard, he managed to shower Naomi in chalk.

"Gracious!" he cried. "I have besmirched your vestments! A thousand apologies!"

He dusted Naomi down as best he could, then bowed his lowest, most repentant bow.

The witch nodded her thanks. Then, as if to acquaint her friend with the predicament, she cast a bleak glance to the knot of children, half in, half out of the door.

Doctor Emberly seemed to immediately comprehend the situation.

"Dear pupils!" he cried. "Brave adventurers on the path of knowledge. Did you think class was cancelled? I can hardly blame you. It's all my own fault for being late. It shall not happen again."

He swept down the room, cooing and tutting and gently ushering bewildered children to their chairs. They were entranced by him, his beaming smile, his irresistible good nature. Even the shy little girl – still firmly gripping Mup's pyjama leg – allowed herself to be guided to a chair.

"Would you like me to sit with you a while?" whispered Mup.

The little girl nodded, her eyes huge over the thumb she'd jammed into her mouth. On the other side of the room Crow was in a similar situation, with two small, grubby boys desperately clutching his coat tails. He smiled triumphantly at Mup as he knelt between the boys' chairs. This is it. *The start of something good.*

All around them children began taking their seats.

At the head of the class Doctor Emberly clapped his ghostly hands, and said:

"Magic is for everyone."

With a gasp, the children looked to Naomi. They obviously expected her to smite the poor doctor. She simply continued to float against the bookshelves, her attention reverently fixed on Emberly's gentle face.

"Magic," said Emberly, "is free."

The children turned wondering eyes back to him.

"We are all born magic," he said. "But we all need to learn how to use that magic. Miss Naomi and I are here to help you do just that — starting with animal transformation."

"Men is ravens," intoned the children. "Women is cats."

"Not any more," said Naomi softly. "Not unless they want to be."

Emberly smiled at her. She smiled back. "Here," said Emberly, "we become whatever we wish to become. Now..." he sparkled a grin at the children, "shall you start by drawing the animal you'd most like to turn into today?"

At Mup's side the little girl's eyes grew wide with excitement. Her thumb popped from her mouth. She released Mup's pyjamas and reached for her pen.

Frog People and the Thirsty Earth

There was a long, quiet time of pencils scratching and papers shuffling. Children began leaning across to see each other's drawings, began borrowing pens, began whispering. When it became obvious that neither Doctor Emberly, drifting luminously up and down between the desks, nor Naomi, glimmering like a marshlight in the darkest corner, minded anyone talking, conversations began to blossom around the room.

Mup's new little friend seemed to quite forget that Mup was by her side, so engrossed did she become in her drawing.

Mup drew back, watching everything. Across the room, Crow bent over a desk, his tousled head the centre of a ring of children who all seemed to be contributing to one large drawing between them. His eyes were still feverishly bright, the shadows under them very dark. In contrast to the plump, merry children around him, Mup thought he looked even thinner than usual.

I think I will ask Fírinne to talk to him, she thought. She wanted to respect her stubborn friend's decision to do things on his own, but as his friend she couldn't help feeling that Crow might need a bit of help. *I'll ask Fírinne to be nice about it, though.* Like Crow himself, the clann leader could be a bit... Well, Fírinne could be a bit gruff. Mup didn't want her two irascible friends to end up fighting.

A sly movement in the corner of her eye brought Mup's attention to the schoolroom door. Two children were standing there, a boy of about twelve and a girl of about five years old: brother and sister, if their looks were anything to go by. They peered into the classroom with wary fascination, the boy holding his little sister firmly by her shoulders as if his wide, flat hands were the only things preventing her from being stolen.

Both had round, wide-featured faces and huge golden eyes.

Where have I seen eyes like that before? wondered Mup.

She stood up, a welcoming smile on her face. The boy, startled that she'd seen him, immediately snatched his sister back and began marching her away up the corridor.

Mup hurried after them. "Won't you come in?" she called.

"Naw," said the boy, still marching.

The little girl looked up at him pleadingly. "But it looks nice in there, Marty."

"We ain't staying. I only come to look-see while Mam was talking."

"But them sprogs was all drawding. I like drawding, me."

The brother began hustling her up the steps. "You can drawd at home." He nodded to Mup. "Sorry to waste your time, ma'am."

"But won't you stay?" she asked. "We're learning magic."

The boy stopped, bringing Mup to a surprised halt on the steps behind him. His eyes flashed angrily in the gloom. "Marshlanders don't need castle lessons," he said. "We have our own magic."

"Oh, Marty!" squeaked his little sister. "Marshlander magic is secret!"

"Not any more it's not," said Marty, and with one last defiant look at Mup, he herded his little sister up the steps, out past Fírinne, and into the courtyard.

Mup went to the door to watch them go. At the boat steps the boy called for attention from whoever stood out of sight below. The familiar voices of Clann'n Cheoil rose up from the riverbed. Their music lifted the children into the air. The little girl squealed and delightedly paddled her feet. The boy looked back at Mup one last time as they were lowered out of sight.

Fírinne, leaning cross-armed in the doorway, quirked an eyebrow at Mup. "They're awkward ones, those Marshlanders. That two give you any trouble?"

Mup shook her head. *Marshlanders*, she thought. *So that's where I've seen their kind before.*

"That boy said his people were here to talk to Mam."

"His mother is one of their leaders. They're down on the riverbed with your mam and dad now, talking about the water situation."

"They don't seem to like the castle much."

Fírinne huffed. "Who does?"

"But when I met Marshlanders before…"

"You met Marshlanders?"

"Yes, the time I got myself thrown in jail. When I was trying to rescue Dad. The two police officers who arrested me were Marshlanders. I know that now because they spoke just like those two kids – that kind of … *bubbling* accent?"

"Oh, yes, the accent's quite distinctive."

"But, Fírinne, the Marshlanders who arrested me seemed … well, they seemed…"

Fírinne crooked a bitter smile. "Obedient?" she asked.

"Yes!" cried Mup.

"The kind of people who would do exactly what the old queen told them, no matter what?"

"*Yes*," agreed Mup. "That boy didn't seem like that at all! Plus, he said they had their own secret magic, Fírinne. The Marshlanders I met wouldn't have had anything to do with secret magic."

"That's what everyone thought," said Fírinne. "The Marshlanders had us all fooled. What a brilliant disguise, hiding under a mask of dullness, while all the time passing their magic skills from one generation to the next. I'd never have thought them capable of it. Mud-brained bog frogs, that's all I thought they were."

"You don't like them very much, do you?"

Fírinne shrugged. "Folk did what they had to to survive under your grandmother's rule," she said. "Still ... it's hard to trust folk who bury their truths so deeply. Hey, where are you going?"

Mup grinned slyly back at her as she made her way across to the boat steps. "I want to hear what's going on."

"That bunch of closed-mouth newts will never help anyone but themselves," grunted Fírinne. "Your mother's wasting her time with them, and you're wasting *your* time if you think they'll say anything worth ear-wigging on."

Mup tutted. "How can you possibly know what

someone will say before they say it? That's just silly." And she put her finger to her lips and crept out of Fírinne's sight down the boat steps.

Heat rose up in waves from the baked surface of the dried riverbed, and sang out unbearably from the stone wall at Mup's back as she slunk down to the last boat step and crouched there, secretly listening to the conversation below. These steps used to lead to the surface of the river, but now that the water level had dropped, they stopped halfway down the castle wall, useless and somehow embarrassed, a flight of stairs to nowhere. *Perfect for spying, though,* thought Mup.

There were two distinct groups of adults on the riverbed. On one side were the Marshlanders, dressed in mossy-looking layers of brown and green. On the other side were Mam and Dad and a selection of the people Mam called her "councillors". Tall and short, spindly and fat, Mam's people were dressed in all the different colours and costumes of the kingdom. Neither group paid any attention to the small dark girl in pyjamas crouched over their heads.

Everyone was sweating in the heat, their attention fixed on a Marshlander man who lay on his stomach at their feet. By his side, a Marshlander woman crouched.

Her broad face was grim beneath the shade of her wide-brimmed hat as she watched the man press his ear to the ground.

"It's a curse, all right," said the man. "You can feel the magic way down there, holding the water in its grip."

The crouching woman nodded her heavy head and looked up at Mam with shrewd golden eyes. "T'aint this bad anywhere else," she said. "Whoever is doing this..."

"My mother is doing this," interrupted Mam.

"Whoever is doing this," repeated the woman, "has concentrated their magic here. They're concentrating on you, and on your castle staff. Trying to thirst you out."

"Can you help us, Marsinda?" asked Dad.

The woman shrugged.

Marsinda, thought Mup. That must be her name.

"You told me that your people have a better understanding of water magic than anyone in the borough," said Mam. "Why go to the bother of telling me that, why come here at all, if you're not willing to help?"

"What do we get for helping?"

Mam frowned. "You get what every citizen of the borough gets. The chance of a better life."

High up on her perch, Mup nodded. That's right. A better life for everyone.

36

Marsinda rose to her feet. "Only a fool gives something for nothing."

"This is your country too," said Dad. "Don't you want to heal it?"

"Everyone here works together," Mam told the woman. "We help each other. Everyone here…"

"Everyone here is out for what they can get!" snapped Marsinda. She pointed to some members of *Clann'n Cheoil*. "That lot have gone from trundling about in boxes on wheels to living in a castle."

"Boxes on wheels?" sputtered a *clann* man. "They're called *vardos*, you ignorant mud-skip! And we don't live in the…"

Ignoring him, the woman gestured to the rest of Mam's councillors. "And these? Ignorant peasants. Grey little bureaucrats. *Merchants*. A motley collection of nothing at all, and all of them suddenly rolling in power and wealth because they took your side."

"That's not—" started Dad.

The woman spoke over him. "I hear you've even got an enforcer here. Absolved of crime. Well, if you can reward one of your mother's pale-faced minions, you can reward the innocent, hardworking people her kind used to trample."

"What is it you need?" asked Mam.

"Need? When a queen takes, is it only what she *needs*? No. It's always what she *wants*."

"I am not a queen," said Mam softly. "But what I want is to heal this land. What is it that *you* want, Marsinda?"

The woman folded her arms. "What are you offering?"

Nothing! thought Mup, incensed by the woman's rudeness and by her greed. *We'll sort this out ourselves!* She launched herself from the boat steps, landed in an angry puff of dust, and began marching toward the delegates.

Unaware of the fuming girl striding her way, Marsinda spoke to the man still crouched at her feet. "Gilborn," she said. "Show this queen what Marshlanders are worth."

The man immediately pressed the tips of his fingers to the ground. His broad face filled first with concentration, then with determination, then – very quickly – with pain.

Mup stopped walking, alarmed at his growing distress.

Gently, his leader put a supportive hand on the man's back. One by one, his people came forward and did the same. "You can do it," murmured Marsinda.

"We're with you," said his friends.

"By grace," whispered one of Mam's councillors. "Look at his fingers."

Mup dropped her attention from the man's agonized expression to the tips of his fingers, still pressed hard to the arid ground. It looked like heat shimmer at first; just a barely perceptible glimmer at his fingertips. Then the ground around his hand darkened. Then it began to gleam. The man's fingers sank into the newly softened earth as water seeped up around them.

"I can't, Marsinda," he gasped as water bubbled up around his hand. "I can't do no more."

"Stop, then," murmured his leader. "Stop. Be at peace."

The man collapsed back into the supporting arms of his companions. Marsinda stepped forward, as if to protect him from the gaping attention of Mam's council. She peered into Mam's face. "What are you offering?" she asked again.

Mam dragged her attention from the gleaming puddle of water at her feet. "Come inside," she said. "Let's talk."

The delegation passed Mup by in a buzz of distraction. Mam and Dad were out of sight at the heart of the group. It wasn't clear to Mup if the others hadn't noticed her, or if she simply wasn't important to them. She didn't mind. She wasn't interested any longer in their conversation, and she certainly wasn't interested in accompanying them inside. She was only interested in the rapidly drying dark patch where the man had pressed his hand to the ground. She crouched and touched her fingertips to it. The ground tingled with ticklish leftover magic. The water was disappearing. Even as Mup held her hands to the dampness, she could feel it being sucked away – down to the dark, lost places where her grandmother's magic held it captive.

No, she thought. *Come back!*

She pressed both hands hard onto the now dry earth, searching desperately for the thin thread of river that the man had somehow been able to guide to the surface. There it was! Receding away, fast, fast, fast! Plummeting down to join the rest of its kind in the darkness.

Mup stretched downwards with her mind. Trying to catch it.

"You'll hurt yourself," called a voice.

Two figures rose to their feet at the base of the castle wall. It was Marty and his little sister. They had been crouched together in the scant shade thrown by the jutting foundations, obviously watching their mother at work. It would seem their people had about as much interest in them as they'd had in Mup, because they had already disappeared into the castle, leaving the children behind.

Marty was hurrying towards her, his little sister trailing anxiously in his wake. "Don't try that on your own!" he warned.

Mup heard the concern in his voice and it just made her angry. She'd show those greedy Marshlanders. She'd do this herself, and then where would they be with their demands?

She returned her attention to the retreating river.

She sent her thoughts after it. *I'm here! Can't you hear me?*

To Mup's amazement, the river did hear her. It *grabbed* for her. Like a falling person might snatch a life rope, the river snatched the part of herself that Mup had sent after it.

It held on, as if clinging to Mup's hand. But Mup wasn't strong enough to prevent the river's fall. Instead of Mup pulling the river up to her, the river dragged Mup down … or rather, it dragged all Mup's moisture with it.

Mup slammed to her hands and knees as every ounce of water in her body tried to follow the river underground. *Let me go!* she thought. But the river, desperate to stop itself plummeting down into the dark, clung mindlessly on.

There came a dreadful *sucking* sensation. Her skin began to shrivel.

Dimly aware of the children running towards her, Mup struggled to free herself from the greedy earth. Her hands were withering. Her arms were getting thin. Mup felt the heart in her chest begin to shrink and waste. She opened her mouth to scream and her breath was nothing but breeze on her dried-out lips.

The boy crouched beside her just as Mup toppled sideways into the dust.

"Help her!" yelled the little girl, hopping from foot to foot behind her brother.

He stared into Mup's eyes as the ground proceeded to suck the moisture from her very blood.

"You can fly," he said.

Mup struggled to speak. "Help ... me..."

The words were barely audible.

"I want to fly," said Marty. "Say you'll teach me, and I'll set you free."

You jerk! thought Mup, rage quite spectacularly overcoming her terror.

The boy must have seen the anger in her eyes. He chuckled, half in admiration, half in scorn.

"You ain't in much position for outrage, ma'am. You're almost dried to a husk. Promise to teach me how to fly and I'll set you free."

Mup's tongue was almost too dry to move. "Join ...

our ... *school*. We'll ... teach ... you ... *everything*..."

The boy sat back in astonishment.

"Marty! Marty!" cried his little sister. "She's turning to dust!"

Mup's sight began to dim. Her eyeballs dried over.

"Marty!" squealed the little girl.

Something cool lay itself on Mup's shoulder, and the link with the cursed river broke with a tangible *ping*. Freshness flowed through Mup as her own moisture returned to fill her out. Drawn up from the ground by the weight of Marty's hand on her shoulder, blood raced through her: plumping the sad, dry, wizened twigs of Mup's arms and legs; filling her heart, her eyes, her brain; rushing joyfully, gleefully, into the empty chambers of her body until she was whole again.

Mup gasped as her lungs filled with air. Her tongue uncleaved itself from the roof of her mouth. She yelled into Marty's face. "You *monster*. Why did you wait so long?"

Marty snatched his hand from her shoulder, stood up, and strode away.

Mup raised herself on shaking arms, watching him go.

"Will you really teach him to fly?" whispered his little sister.

"Of course," Mup rasped. "He didn't have to try and force me. That's what school is for. We teach anyone who wants to learn."

"Even me?" The little girl's eyes grew even larger. "But I ain't important!"

Mup dragged herself to her feet, leaning on the little girl's shoulder.

"What's your name?" she rasped.

"Grislet."

"Grislet, everyone is important. Just … just come to Mam's school, OK? Come to school and we'll teach you anything you want to learn." She glanced over to Marty, who lurked uncertainly in the shadow of the castle. "He looks scared."

"Aye. He's afraid he'll be punished."

"For what? He *saved* me."

"Aye, but he didn't get a payment for it."

"Oh, *come on!*" cried Mup.

The little girl shook her head at Mup's innocence. "I like you, ma'am," she said unexpectedly. "You smell nice. You've got pretty colours on you."

"Um … thank you."

"But you're *castle folk*, ma'am. Our mam says that no castle bully will ever take anything from us again – not without paying first. If our mam finds out Marty helped you without getting something in return. Well…" Her rueful shrug left the consequences of Marty's actions unspoken but clearly suggested.

Mup bent to look into the little girl's golden eyes. "I won't tell on your brother," she promised.

"And?"

"And what?" asked Mup.

"And what do you want in return?"

Mup sighed. "Nothing, Grislet. I don't want anything in return."

She began wobbling her way back to the castle. After a few unsteady steps, she was startled by the cool, damp feel of Grislet's arm slipping around her waist. The little girl said nothing, just supported some of Mup's weight. Mup wasn't stupid enough to say thank you. They walked on.

"I'm not castle folk, you know, Grislet."

The golden eyes flashed her way, just briefly, a small, sarcastic look.

"Really," insisted Mup. "I'm just an ordinary person."

"You live in a castle, ma'am. Your mother be the queen. Your *grandmother* was the queen."

"But…"

"You're castle folk, ma'am," said Grislet.

Her tone was so flat, so matter-of-fact, that Mup

stopped talking. What was she trying to prove by insisting she wasn't a castle person? Was she trying to pretend that she was just like Marty and Grislet? She wasn't like them. She hadn't had to live their lives. They were not and never would be the same. *It doesn't matter*, thought Mup, squeezing Grislet's shoulder. *It doesn't matter how different we are. We'll find a way to work together.*

The castle foundations rose high above the riverbed like a sheer cliff. The steps seemed miles away, and Mup eyed them with despair. She wasn't sure how she was going to manage getting back inside. She didn't feel particularly able to walk, let alone fly.

As they approached, Marty stuck out his arm and Grislet slipped to his side. His eyes stayed on the ground the whole time. "Let's go in to Mam," he mumbled.

Grislet slid a look to Mup. "Are we allowed to *you-know-what* in front of *you-know-who?*"

Marty raised his chin. "Free people can do whatever they like, Grislet. Come on."

Quick as a shimmer, Marty and Grislet transformed. It took Mup a moment to understand exactly what had happened. She was so used to seeing people transform into cats and ravens, that her mind did not register what she'd seen. At first she thought they'd just disappeared.

But then a small, sand-coloured lizard ran up the wall by her side. It was joined by another even smaller lizard.

They clung there for a moment, staring at Mup with big, golden eyes. Then the bigger one said, "I won't help you again, ma'am. If you're reckless enough to commune with betrapped water, you'll be on your own."

With a flick of his tail, Marty skittered away up the wall.

His little sister blinked at Mup. "He's actually very nice," she whispered. "He'd never really let you turn to dust." She hurried after her brother.

The two little lizards scaled the wall with no effort at all. Soon they were at the top, over the edge, into the courtyard and out of sight. Mup was left alone in the heat, feeling like someone had wrung her like a rag, and hung her out to dry.

Dark Music, Grey Girl

Mup managed to float to the top of the boat steps and stumble into the yard. She was so tired she felt broken, so dry her eyeballs felt like sand. There was no sign of Marty and Grislet. Mup wondered how they expected to find their way in the great imposing labyrinth of the palace. Fírinne was no longer guarding the schoolroom door. Perhaps she'd taken them to their parents?

The empty courtyard was very still, the only movement the constant scrolling of the memorial wall at the back of the yard. Had Marty seen the names? Grislet was too young yet to see them – to her the wall would just be a wall. But surely Marty was old enough?

No doubt the sight of it had brought him to a halt for a moment – as it did everyone who came to the castle. *What had he made of it?* Mup wondered. What had his mother and her councillors made of it, and of Mam's

48

insistence that it be here, visible to any who visited, the open acknowledgement of all the harm perpetrated under the old queen?

Happy voices filtered through the stillness, the shrieks and laughter of children at play. Mup smiled as she realized the boisterous sounds were combined with barking and hooting and – was that the trumpeting of an elephant? She laughed. What had Emberly and Naomi let themselves in for? She wobbled her way towards the guardroom, ready for a sit-down, more than ready for a long cool drink of water.

She was only halfway across the yard when Naomi appeared in the inky rectangle of the guardroom door. There came a shimmer behind her, a fizz of colour. With a gasp of wonder, Mup saw that the guardroom had filled with butterflies. Naomi paused in the doorway. The butterflies gathered around her. For a moment the ghost's pale face and dark hair were haloed in a riot of colour. Then the butterflies fluttered past her and out into the sunshine.

One of the butterflies flew right up to Mup. "Hello!" it said, in a faint but instantly recognizable voice. It was the little girl who had been so scared earlier! "Do you like my new colours?" The butterfly spun in the air. "My sister says that butterflies are useless, but Doctor Emberly says, 'we must simply enjoy being ourselves without seeking other people's...' Um... 'other people's...'"

"'APPROVAL!'" chorused the rest of the butterflies.

They clustered around. Delighted, Mup lifted her hand, and her little friend landed on her finger. The others landed on Mup's hair and shoulders and face, laughing and chattering, and singing together in tiny voices.

Naomi spoke above the chatter. "Go back to the garden now. In where it is safe."

The butterflies rose in a giggling cloud and streamed past her into the darkness of the castle. Naomi watched after them, as if waiting for them to pass into safety.

The happy sounds from inside swelled as the butterflies rejoined their school mates.

"Is that *really* an elephant trumpeting?" laughed Mup.

But her amusement died at Naomi's frowning look. "What has happened out here?" asked the witch. "I felt... I don't know what I felt. An unpleasantness. A *darkening*. Was it you?"

Mup was tempted to lie, but the ghost's expression brooked no evasions, so she told Naomi everything. Naomi's habitual coolness softened somewhat.

"That was an extremely foolish thing to do," she murmured.

"I'm sorry. I thought I could make a path to the water. I thought..."

50

"You thought you could perform magic that not even your mother is capable of."

"Please don't tell Mam."

"Children must not play with curses."

"I *wasn't* playing."

The ghost bent to look Mup in the eye. She spoke every word with stern emphasis. "You *cannot* fight your grandmother's magic alone. None of us can. *Promise* me you won't try such a thing again."

Mup looked away. "I... I need to lie down, Naomi."

She waited for Naomi to once again request a promise. But the ghost simply sighed, straightened, and let the subject go. "The students are at break," she said. "They shall be fine under Doctor Emberly's supervision. I shall take the time to bring you and Crow to your room where you can sleep off your recklessness."

"Crow's not with me! Isn't he inside?"

Naomi frowned. "He left when break started. I had assumed you were together."

"No."

"Perhaps he has gone to his vardo."

The vardo. That song. That crawling darkness.

"Naomi, have you noticed anything strange about Crow recently?"

"If I am perfectly honest, I find most children strange."

Mup sighed. Naomi eyed her shrewdly.

"But, do you perhaps mean the shadows that our friend has begun to inadvertently trail around after him?"

Startled, Mup met the witch's gaze.

"Perhaps you are not the only one playing with powerful magic," said Naomi quietly. "Do you suppose Crow might need some advice?"

"Maybe."

"From me?"

"Um…"

Naomi folded her hands. "I understand," she said. "He does not trust me."

"No!" hurried Mup. "It's just…" She gestured at Naomi's clothes. "Naomi … couldn't you do something about the uniform? Change into a less … upsetting outfit?"

"I cannot. I died in this uniform; it is mine forever. But, in truth, even had I a choice I do not think I would change my appearance. Other clothes would only serve to hide what I had been, what I allowed to be done to others. I will not run from the rightful disapprobation of those who suffered at the hands of my kind."

"But you were just a kid when you were made join the raggedy witches! You had no choice!"

"I have a choice now. I choose to atone."

Mup couldn't think of what to say to that.

Naomi turned away. "You fly up to Crow's camp. I will meet you there."

"You're taking the stairs?" asked Mup, already knowing the answer.

"Of course."

"Wouldn't it be quicker to fly?"

Naomi turned back. Her expression told Mup that she was weary of this conversation, but was willing to have it as many times as necessary until people got the point. "In life, I stood by as others suffered, Mup. I allowed others to die, all so that I might be granted the opportunity to use my own magic. Do you understand?"

Mup nodded.

"I will never use magic again," said Naomi. She turned away once more. "Fly up to Crow. I will join you as soon as I am able. If our friend is willing to accept my advice, I shall give it to him. If not, we will find someone less tainted to help him."

Mup felt the darkness before she'd even cleared the edge of the roof. She heard the song too, drifting like a shadow under the scent of thyme blossom and early hyacinth. She rose above the level of the parapet. There was dread in her heart, but she was prepared now, as she hadn't been before, for the tangle of power that permeated the sunny roof garden.

Oh, Crow, she thought. *What are you doing?*

Was this why her friend insisted on being alone? Was this why he lived so far from everyone?

Still floating, Mup curled her fingers around the edge of the parapet and listened. Crow's song snaked around the vardo, weaving in and out, up and down. His words were unintelligible: Mup was not a hundred per cent certain that they even *were* words. Perhaps Crow was simply making sounds – allowing his heart to speak into the music without any constraint. Her eyes could not see the magic Crow's song invoked, but her heart could feel it, and it was *dark*.

Carefully, Mup reached across the parapet and pressed her palm to the flat of the roof. *Show me*, she thought.

The caravan seethed in shadows. Its colours flickered on and off, on and off, colour and grey, colour and grey, as if the vardo was hopping between two places or hopping between two times – night and day, maybe, life and death, heaven and...

Mup snatched her hand away.

The roof garden snapped back into focus. The shadows retreated to their place.

All except one.

Crouched in the dark pool of shade beneath the vardo hunched a small, unhappy shape. Mup startled, as she realized the shape was a person. Then she frowned as she realized she knew who the person was. Angry, Mup crawled over the parapet. She waded through the seething magic that surrounded the vardo. She got down on her hands and knees in the fizzing torment of air and met the anguished eyes of the little grey girl.

"What are you *doing?*" Mup hissed. "You're to leave Crow alone, you hear me?"

The ghost actually jumped. She shielded her face with her hands. She tried to crawl away. Mup's anger melted. The poor creature was utterly confused.

"I'm sorry," said Mup. "For a minute I thought you were causing this. But you're not, are you? It's Crow."

Crow's song, seeping down from vardo above them, changed pitch and the poor ghost gasped. She shook her head. She covered her ears.

"Crow!" yelled Mup, hammering her fist on the bottom of the vardo. "Crow, stop singing!"

Silence crashed down around them. There came a series of startled noises from above.

Mup reached in between the wheels and took the grey girl's hand. "It's OK," she soothed. "He's stopped."

Overhead, the vardo door banged open. Crow clattered down the steps.

The little grey girl squinted around, as if only now aware of where she was. She moaned in disgust. She flung herself backwards, and Mup – still clinging to the girl's hand – was dragged with her into the dark.

There came a horrible, squashing, stretching feeling, as if Mup was made of jelly and someone was dragging her through a keyhole. For a brief, dreadful moment, bits of her got very narrow, bits of her got very wide and all of her was very uncomfortable. Then she was out the other side and zooming through air, still clutching tightly to the grey girl's hand.

"Stop!" she cried. "Stop!"

They stumbled to a halt, staggering together in the dimness.

Mup felt strange: there and not there, stretched like a bit of elastic.

Then everything twanged back together and she felt surprisingly all right again.

"Where are we?" She looked around. They were in an endless corridor of smooth walls and floor. Everything seemed to be made of mist. Far off, down at the very end of the corridor, a gentle light glowed. Overhead, the low ceiling was soft and drifting, like cloud. The floor flowed and rippled beneath Mup's feet, like a river of fog. "Where are we?" she asked again.

The grey girl was standing with her hands folded on her ashy chest, a look of relief on her face. At Mup's repeated question, she smiled. "Home," she breathed, in her raspy, unused voice.

"Home? This ... this is where you live now?"

"Sleep," murmured the girl, laying herself down into the fog.

"Wait!" cried Mup. The little girl seemed to be blending with the floor. She was disappearing into the mist! "Wait! Don't leave me! I don't know where I am!"

The girl roused herself, grouchily lifting her head from the flowing grey. "This is a sleeping place," she insisted. "Why do you keep waking me? I am not..." She seemed to realize for the first time that she was talking to Mup. Her bright, black eyes shot wide in horror. "What are you doing here?" she rasped. "You're not dead."

"Well, I should hope not!" said Mup.

The girl rushed to her feet in a swirl of fog. "Stop that!" she cried.

"Stop what?" Mup looked down at herself in alarm. Her body was a mass of shimmering gold. "Oh, goodness. I'm all shiny!" She held her hands to her face, and she could see right through them, as if she were made of glitter and honey. "How lovely!"

"Not lovely!" growled the girl. "You're *alive*. Alive persons are *bad* for the ghost place. Too shiny: hurting our eyes with glittering! Too noisy: waking us up with singing!"

"It wasn't *me* singing," said Mup. "It was Crow. And let's face it, I hadn't much choice about coming to the ... the ghost place. You *dragged* me here."

The grey girl growled again. She spun Mup on her heel. "Look!"

A tunnel of mist opened at the command of the girl's pointed finger.

There were figures at the far end of it, moving frantically.

"Listen!" rasped the girl.

Voices came faintly through: panic-stricken, angry, afraid.

"Who is that?" whispered Mup.

The girl hissed urgently in her ear. "Tell the boy to stop rousing the dead!"

"What?"

The girl pushed Mup hard between her shoulder blades. The tunnel of fog opened like a rose, and Mup fell into it. She tumbled towards the voices, the words getting clearer as the distant figures moved against the light.

"She's dead! Mup's dead!" *Was that Crow?*

"How did this happen, boy?" *Fírinne – shouting.*

"She was on the ground when I came out! She called me and I came out and there she was!"

Naomi's voice, paper-thin compared to the others. "She had been unwell in the courtyard."

"Why did you leave her alone, then?" yelled Fírinne.

Mup tumbled and spun, and the figures came clear through the mist.

Oh, look! she thought in surprise. *There I am!*

And there she was indeed, lying on the ground as the others bent over her.

I do look quite dead, she thought.

Crow wrung his hands, his face wet with tears. "Save her, Fírinne!"

A great shadow swooped over everything, and Mup knew Mam had just landed on the roof.

But there was no more time for looking and listening because Mup was zooming down through colours. She was tumbling down through hot air. There was a brief, alarming close-up of her own face, slack and dead-looking, surrounded by the soft cloud of her hair: then BAM! she was heavier than clay: and SLAM! her heart was tripping like a hammer: and *GASP!* she was trying to suck in air.

It all got very confusing then, and Mup's concentration was entirely taken up with reminding her lungs how to breathe and reminding her heart how to beat, and everything else disappeared for quite a while.

Something Wicked

Voices wavered in and out.

"She's very ill…" Doctor Emberly.

"What type of ill? Normal-type ill? Magic-type ill?" Dad.

"Well … temporarily-dead type of ill, I think."

"Dead!"

"Only temporarily dead … as far as I can tell."

"AS FAR AS YOU CAN TELL?"

Mam's voice broke gently in on Dad's panic. "Daniel, let's you, me and the doctor have this talk outside."

Crow came and sat on Mup's bed, staring down at her with horribly wide eyes.

Mup very much wanted to smile at him and say, Hey! I'm fine! But her brain didn't seem wired up right and she just lay like a log against her pillows while tears flowed silently down her friend's face and dripped off his chin.

"I'm sorry," he whispered. "I'm sorry."

Oh, Crow, she thought. It's OK!

But Crow left without Mup being able to move so much as a muscle to comfort him. Not even Tipper's cold wet nose or Badger's snuffling kisses could get her mind and her body connected again. Everyone left, and she lay looking at the ceiling and listening to the curtains blow in the hot breeze, absolutely incapable of moving.

This is terribly frustrating, she thought. Wait till I see that grey girl again. I'll give her a piece of my mind.

"You're not dead," rasped a familiar rusty voice at the end of the bed.

Mup strained her eyes to see.

The grey girl was glowering from over the footboard. "You're not dead," she rasped again.

I know that! thought Mup.

"Why do you not move?"

I can't!

The grey girl came up the side of the bed.

"Get up!" she growled and slapped Mup's forehead.

"OW!" Mup sat up with a jerk, her hands clapped to her head. "What did you do that for?"

"Need to show you something."

"Oh, hey! I can move again!"

"A bad thing is coming," muttered the girl.

Alarmed, Mup slipped from bed. "What bad thing? Where?"

"A bad thing, from a bad time..." The girl dropped to her knees and began scrawling on the floor. "Minion..." she said. "Enforcer..."

"You mean a raggedy witch? A raggedy witch is coming?" Mup knelt beside the girl, staring at her indecipherable squiggles. "I ... I can't tell what that is."

"I'll take you," muttered the girl, scrawling feverishly. "Show you..."

"Can't you just tell me?"

Impatiently, the grey girl grabbed Mup's hand. She slapped it palm first onto the ashy scribble on the floor. Suddenly they were inside Crow's vardo, everything streaming grey. Crow was cooking and singing softly to himself, his home neat and lovely all around him.

"Is this where the bad thing is?" whispered Mup.

The grey girl grimaced. It seemed this was not where she had intended to bring Mup.

"This is not important," she growled. "Follow." She began dragging Mup away.

"Wait." Mup twisted to keep Crow in sight. "Is this happening now?"

Her friend continued singing as if they weren't there. He was giving the tune no thought. It just came out of him, sad and sweet, the unconscious expression of his heart. As he sang, a shape began to form behind him. Mup could see that it was being gathered from the shadows of the vardo – called forth by Crow's voice. Hunched and misshapen, it coalesced behind her unsuspecting friend.

Mup yelled a warning. "Crow! Look out!"

But Crow just kept singing, unaware of what his music was doing.

The figure rose up behind him, its half formed features dreadful. It staggered, clumsy and unsure. "Whuh?" it gurgled. "Whaah?"

"We have to help Crow!" cried Mup.

"This is not IMPORTANT!" shouted the grey girl. She slapped Mup's forehead again, and they were zooming through greyness.

"You can't keep doing that to me!" howled Mup.

Down passageways they zoomed, and over water. Then – BAM – they were out in the open air, on the edge of a cliff.

There was a woman there, her hair streaming out in the westerly wind. Her pale face was calm as she contemplated the sea, which stretched all the way to a distant horizon. Mup almost didn't recognize her because of her clothes and expression. Then she realized it was Magda. It was Crow's mother: looking comfortable and ordinary in trousers and cardigan; looking peaceful and content.

"Bad," growled the grey girl in Mup's ear.

"Yes, very bad..."

Magda turned from them. She walked up a narrow path to a tiny house.

The grey girl pushed Mup and they followed behind, floating like mist up the path, then passing like mist through the door that Magda had closed behind her. It was an ordinary kitchen, and Magda drifted around it doing ordinary things. She filled a kettle. She put on a radio. There were potted geraniums on the windowsills. There was a tiger-striped cat on a chair. Mup realized this was the mundane world. "Is this now?" she whispered. "Is this happening now?"

The girl didn't answer and Mup thought she maybe did not know.

Magda hummed to herself as she pottered about.

She's singing the same tune as Crow, thought Mup. *Are they singing at the same time?* She shivered, again feeling the strength of Crow's song. Even across this distance of time and space, it seemed to cast a powerful influence.

Magda bent to her geraniums. Smiling, she pinched a dead leaf from an otherwise healthy stem. "Aren't you pretty?" she murmured to the plant. "Aren't you..."

She stopped talking.

She withdrew her hand.

Mup could not understand the horror that passed across Magda's face. Had she seen a slug?

And, just like that, the plant collapsed into a pile of ash.

"What ... what's happening?" whispered Mup.

Magda released a strangled cry. She rushed to another pot plant. She cupped her hands around its scarlet blossoms. For a moment nothing happened. Her face filled with hope. Then the plant fell away in a puff of ash. Magda whirled around, her hands poised. She saw a book by the fireplace, resting on a colourful blanket. She ran to these things and grabbed them. They exploded into ash. She raced to the table. She snatched a yellow bowl. Cracks splintered its surface. It too fell away.

Wide-eyed, Magda pressed her back to the wall. "But this is mine," she whispered. "It's mine."

A soft mewing froze her. The tiger-striped cat had jumped from its chair. Perhaps hoping to comfort its mistress, perhaps hoping for her to comfort it, it slunk across the floor, and flowed a purring figure of eight against Magda's legs.

Magda closed her eyes. "No," she whispered. "No. Please."

But the purring stopped. When Magda looked down there was no more cat, just a soft drift of ashes coating the leather of her boots.

"Oh, no!" yelled Mup in horror.

Magda looked up sharply, as if hearing her.

Mup and the grey girl shrank back as the witch locked eyes with Mup.

"You promised me," hissed Magda.

Mup raised her hands as if to deny she'd ever made such a promise.

Magda stalked vengefully forward. "You promised I'd be forgiven."

"I … I never…" stumbled Mup. "I never."

The grey girl's fingers tightened on Mup's shoulders as Magda loomed, but the woman stalked right through them. For a moment Mup's vision was blinded and her breath stuttered by the witch's dark passing, then she was out in the garden, watching as Magda stormed out of the front door of her little house.

Magda slammed the door behind her with all the finality of goodbye. The house exploded into ash. Magda did not even flinch. The garden gate fell into ashes at the touch of her hand. All the fence posts which ringed her pretty garden puffed apart. Magda was already striding away. She did not look back as, one by one, her well-tended plants and flowers and fruit trees gave themselves up in gritty clouds to the tumultuous sky.

Sailing high above, Mup and the grey girl followed Magda's tall, spare figure as she strode across the landscape. Trees and bushes and unsuspecting little animals burst to ashes as she passed. On the horizon a border glittered. Beyond it a land, already suffering under its own curse, burned and sweltered under a cloudless sky. The witch stormed towards it, trailing darkness like a long grey cloak.

"Where is she going?" whispered Mup, the answer already dreadfully clear.

"Home," whispered the grey girl.

"I need to get back! I need to warn them!"

The grey girl smacked her forehead and Mup bolted upright in bed, screaming for Mam.

Family

"We lock the castle down," snarled Mam. "I want guards on every parapet. I want ravens on every windowsill. Call back the men and women who are out hunting for my mother. Bring everyone inside the walls. *Everyone*."

Her guards snapped brisk salutes and rushed away.

Dad closed the apartment door behind them, and Mam turned to Mup, who was huddled, all shivery, in a blanket on the sofa. Tipper and Badger lay at Mup's feet. Crow lurked by the window, unhappy and fretful in his boy form. Mup kept trying to catch his eye but he wouldn't look at her.

"Tell me more about your vision, Mup," said Mam, coming to kneel in front of her.

"There's nothing more to tell, Mam."

"Is that woman far away? Could she still be in the mundane world?"

"I don't know, Mam. I don't think the grey girl understands time. She could have been showing me the past, the future or the present. All I know is she was showing me the truth."

Mup glanced again at Crow, thinking of the dark figure in his vardo. *Past or future?* she wondered. Was the creature something that might happen? Or was it already there?

"Your hands are so cold, Mup," said Mam.

"Me and Badger is warming her feets," piped Tipper from his position on the floor.

Mup wiggled her toes against his furry belly so that he giggled. At the same time she gazed at Mam. "Will we have to fight Magda?"

"Hopefully it won't come to that."

"That *damn* woman," muttered Fírinne. "Why would she come here?"

As if in answer to this, every adult in the room turned to Crow. He shrank back against the curtains. Mup was certain he'd turn into a raven right there and then, and fly away. She was just about to point out that Crow had nothing to do with Magda, that she'd never wanted any contact with her son, when Fírinne surprised her by striding across the room. To Crow's obvious alarm, the tall woman crouched, gripped his shoulder, and looked him fiercely in the eye.

"Don't worry, boy," she said. "Whatever your mother's intentions, we won't let her near you."

Crow didn't seem to know what to say. Eventually he managed an astonished little "thanks".

Fírinne slapped his arm in gruff sympathy, and turned to Mam. "What do we do about the school children?"

"It'd be safest to keep them here," said Dad.

"You know what that would look like to their parents," said Fírinne. "The first people to risk sending their children here, and we hold them captive in the castle?"

Mam groaned. "Could this have happened on a worse day?"

Dad looked gently at her. "You're the most powerful weapon these people have, Stella." He held up a hand to stop her objections. "I know you don't want to be thought of as that. But there's no avoiding it. Next to your mother, you're the most powerful weapon there is. You should accompany those children home."

Mam got to her feet. "I'm not leaving you and the kids, Daniel."

"We're as safe as houses here."

"I'm not leaving you."

"We made a commitment to those children when we opened that school. We promised their parents we'd keep

71

them safe. You need to fulfil that promise, otherwise..."
Dad spread his hands. "Otherwise, it's all just words."

Mam sighed. "Why must you always talk sense?" She went and took Dad's face in her hands. "You'll stay right here?"

"I won't budge an inch."

Mam kissed him on the mouth.

She turned to Mup. "As for you, Mup Taylor! No more big magic. No more going it alone."

Mup tiredly raised her hands in surrender. "I promise," she whispered.

"And if that grey girl shows up again...?"

"I'll spit in her eye."

Mam knelt down by Tipper. "Give your mammy a kiss." Tipper licked her nose. "A proper kiss, you chancer." He turned into a little boy, plopped a kiss on her cheek, and flopped straight back down into a puppy again. Mam scrubbed his ears, stood, and looked at Crow. He glanced at her sideways from his position by the curtains. "I care about you, Crow," she said.

His dark eyes shot to her face. He seemed shocked beyond words.

"Stay with the family, OK? I need to know you're safe."

Crow swallowed hard. Mup thought he might be on

the verge of speaking. But the raven guard chose that moment to caw its presence, the sky outside darkened with the shiver of wings, and Crow retreated into silence.

"We'd best go," said Mam.

Fírinne nodded grimly, shook herself, and transformed into a silver raven. With a flutter of wings, she hopped to the table, then out onto the windowsill.

There came a great sweep of movement beside Mup. She turned just in time to see a huge raven launch itself into the air. Mam, she thought, as the raven glided overhead. For a moment Mam's wings filled the window, then she landed at Fírinne's side. The setting sun gleamed on her noble beak, and glinted fire in her eyes as she scanned the courtyard below. Beside her, Fírinne threw back her head and called, harsh and loud, to the amassing birds.

There was a vast uprush of wings, a welter of shadow flickered the room, and Mam and Fírinne were gone.

Mup struggled from the sofa. She and Tipper crowded at the window to watch. Crow came quietly to their side. Down below, the children were gathered in the bruised shadows of the evening yard. They were very different to how they'd been this morning. Most of them laughed as they chatted together. Some linked arms, some sang. Many of them waved up to Mup in her distant sunlit window. "Hope you feel better, Mup! See you soon, Crow!"

Naomi and Emberly were with them, gazing skywards, anxiety clear on their luminous faces. Mam and Fírinne swooped down to join them. There was a brief exchange of words, and the children began making for the boat steps.

From her advantage high above everything, Mup could see Marsinda near the back of the yard, watching the activity with frowning intensity. Where the rest of the Marshlanders were, Mup did not know; somewhere in the castle, she supposed. Mam had asked them to stay, at least until she knew what threat Magda might pose.

The Marshlander leader couldn't take her eyes from Naomi. She stared as the ghost gently ushered the children to the steps, stared as Naomi anxiously waved them off on their journey home.

Mup thought Marsinda seemed very different to the brash woman of that morning. It was obvious that Naomi's presence stirred dreadful memories. Once again, Mup wished that her ghostly friend could change her appearance. Whatever Mup's feelings about Marsinda, it couldn't be pleasant for people like her – or Doctor Emberly for that matter – to be confronted with the walking symbol of all their past sufferings.

Unaware of the Marshlander's presence, Naomi and Emberly crossed the yard together, heading for an inner door.

"You have no right," yelled Marsinda suddenly.

The two ghosts came to a startled halt.

Marsinda pointed a shaking finger at Naomi. "You have no right to the company of our children. You have no right to respect and decency when every memory we have of you burns like fire."

Mup saw Emberly step forward as if to speak. Naomi put her hand on his ghostly arm.

"What you say is true," she told Marsinda. "I'm sorry."

"If I were you I'd lock myself away where no one would have to suffer the sight of me."

"As soon as there are enough teachers for the school, I will do just that."

Marsinda didn't seem to know what to do with that information. Naomi bowed to her. The gesture seemed to bring Marsinda only greater pain and upset. When Naomi left the courtyard, the Marshlander leader collapsed a little bit in on herself – shrank.

Emberly spoke in quiet sympathy. "Are you all right?"

His voice snapped Marsinda's spine straight again. "Did you die by their hands?" she growled.

Emberly nodded. "Under torture."

That seemed to take Marsinda back. She stared at Emberly, as if seeing him anew. "How have you not gone insane working with that creature every day? Having to look at it every day?"

"I try not to think of Naomi as a 'creature'," said Emberly softly. "I try to think of her as a child, wrapped in a uniform she deeply regrets, trying to atone for sins that are not entirely her own." He hesitated. "But if I am honest ... some days the sight of her is almost too much for me to bear."

Dad placed his hands on Mup's shoulders. She realized that, though Crow and Tipper had left the window as soon as the school-children had disappeared from view, Dad had remained with her, listening to the conversation below. His dark eyes followed Emberly as the ghost left the courtyard.

Marsinda stayed by the memory wall, her arms folded tight as if to keep herself safe.

Dad squeezed Mup's shoulders. "Come inside, Mup."

"I don't know who to feel sorry for," whispered Mup. "Naomi or Marsinda. I don't know whose side I'm on."

Dad looked down at her with his kind smile. "You don't have to take sides," he said. "In a situation like this, maybe all you can do is listen, and try to understand ...

and give everyone room to figure out the answers for themselves."

"Get some rest now," said Dad, tucking Mup into bed. "Doctor Emberly says you're still not well."

Crow lurked at the door. Dad ruffled his hair as he left the room. "Don't tire her out, fella."

Dad went out to read Tipper a story. Crow came and sat cross-legged at the end of Mup's bed. He listened as Dad's voice and Tipper's voice rose up in the sitting room. When it was clear that they were fully occupied with reading Tipper's choo-choo book, Crow whispered:

"You look terrible, Mup."

"Thanks a million."

"All grey and limp."

"I feel grey and limp to be honest."

Crow fidgeted with the bed covers. "Was it my singing did that to you?"

"Don't think so. Think it was the grey girl dragging me into the ghost place did this to me."

This didn't seem to comfort Crow much. He kept fidgeting with the bedclothes and glancing up at the ceiling as if there was something up there he was worried about.

"Are you worried about your vardo, Crow?"

He stared at her, frozen and wary.

"Are you worried about what might be in the vardo?"

This was like releasing a spring inside her friend, and he immediately crawled to her end of the bed, his eyes wide, his expression filled with relief and urgency. "Oh, Mup," he whispered. "I don't know what to do. He just appeared and then he fell over and he seems so sad."

Mup sat straighter, gripping her friend's hands tight. "What is he?"

"I don't know! He's not a ghost. He's certainly not a person!"

"When did he appear, Crow?"

"This morning! I went up to cook my middle-breakfast while class was at break." Crow searched his memory, trying to get the whole fuddled morning into place. "I was *cooking*," he whispered, "and..."

"And you were singing to yourself," said Mup. "That's what woke the grey girl. She told me."

"My *singing* woke the girl?"

Mup nodded. "She was asleep until then, apparently."

"I was singing to myself..." whispered Crow. "And I heard a noise behind me, and *there he was*, gurgling and staggering about. And then you called me, and I ran out and..." He shook his head, obviously not wanting to think about finding Mup lying there, dead on the ground. "I thought I'd killed you, Mup."

She smiled. "Well ... you hadn't. Is your creature still there, do you think? Maybe he went away when you stopped singing?"

Crow shook his head, not knowing.

Mup slipped from bed, and staggered for the sitting room.

"I don't want to go back there alone," whispered Crow.

Surprised, Mup turned at the door. "Why would you go alone, Crow? You're part of a family. You have people who care about you." She held out her hand for him. "You don't have to do anything alone."

A Mother's Return

"Your mother is going to kill me," grunted Dad, pushing his broad shoulders through the attic window.

"Tipper will probably kill you first. He's not at all happy we left him behind with Naomi."

"We could hardly bring the little fellow with us," observed Doctor Emberly, floating up through the roof tiles at Mup's feet. "He's still terribly young, you know — even in dog years."

"Are you all right, Mup?" asked Dad. "You're very grey about the gills."

Mup was standing with Crow on the apex of the roof, patiently waiting for Dad to squeeze his way through the window. She sighed. "I'd quite like to never be dead again, thank you."

Doctor Emberly seemed a bit offended at that. "Well," he sniffed. "It takes a lot out of the living, I suppose."

The raven guard wheeled protective circles overhead as Dad scrambled to the ridge of the roof. He frowned up at them, his shadow stretched far behind him, his face glowing in the setting sun. He nodded at Crow. "Right," he said. "Guards or not, I don't want any of us out here longer than necessary. Let's go check on your creature."

"He's not my creature," grumbled Crow, leading the way across the ridge tiles.

"I beg to differ," interjected Doctor Emberly. "If – as you surmise – you conjured him with your voice, he's very much your creature, and as such you have quite a responsibility for his well-being."

"But I didn't mean to conjure him, did I? I didn't even know I was singing. I was just humming away to myself, cooking my middle-breakfast, and having a little think."

The doctor faltered, as if something had just fallen into place for him. "Crow…" he ventured. "Crow, was there anyone in particular on your mind when you were, um … 'humming away to yourself' and 'having a little think'?"

Crow came to an abrupt halt, causing the row of friends to bang into each other in a small series of "sorry"s and "do excuse me"s. He stood with his back to them all for a moment, the sunset haloing his tousled head, his arms out for balance. His vardo was in sight now.

81

Crow ran a few steps towards it, and then – even though they'd agreed that Dad wouldn't be left behind – he leapt into his raven form and flew the last bit of distance by himself.

"Oh dear," whispered Emberly. "That poor child."

"Why?" asked Mup. "Who is it you think was on his mind?"

"My dear princess," said Emberly. "Whom does an orphan child *always* have on their mind? To whom does the orphan's lonely heart turn at every quiet moment?"

"Oh, no," whispered Dad, apparently understanding Doctor Emberly far better than Mup did.

Crow had already landed on his roof garden. Mup turned to see him rise into his boy form and run for the vardo. "Crow!" she shouted. "Wait for us! *Don't do this on your own.*"

"Fly to him," said Dad. "I'll catch up."

Mup launched and flew and landed at the bottom of the vardo steps just as Crow reached the porch. He hesitated with his hand on the door handle, panting. Mup was able to run up the steps and be at his side when he opened the door, and witnessed what lay within.

The little grey girl was there, and she turned to look at them as dying light streamed into the vardo. The creature was kneeling by her side, hunched and misshapen, its head bowed onto the grey girl's chest. Its broad shoulders were almost half the width of the vardo. If it rose to its feet, it would be too tall to stand straight. The grey girl was stroking its matted hair with her ashy hand. She threw Crow such an accusing glare that Mup wanted to put her arm around him, to protect him from it.

You've no right to look at Crow that way! she thought. *Not after all the things you've done.*

The girl glanced at her, and maybe she saw something of this in Mup's expression, because she dropped her gaze and went back to stroking the creature's hair.

"Poor sad, hurting thing," she rasped. "It doesn't know what it is."

"It's my dad," whispered Crow.

"What?" cried Mup.

Crow didn't look at her. He stepped into the vardo, his eyes on the creature kneeling at the grey girl's feet. "My dad didn't look like that, though," he whispered.

"You do not remember him as well as you think, maybe," said the girl, some sympathy in her fierceness now. "Or you didn't concentrate enough. So –" she gestured to the creature – "he is not complete."

"But Crow's singing called you up," said Mup to the little girl. "You're complete!"

"Boy's song didn't *conjure* me. Boy only woke me.

83

I heard his music, because I'm always close, I'm always listening even when I sleep. But Boy wasn't singing for me."

"I wasn't singing for anyone," whispered Crow. "I was only singing for myself, and remembering Dad, and…" He went to touch the creature. "Oh, Dad, it really is you, isn't it?"

The sky outside darkened. Urgent cawing filled the air. Mup turned to see the cloud of raven guard swoop low as Dad and Emberly frantically ran towards her. "We need to get back inside!" yelled Dad. "Hurry!" His eyes were on the sky. Emberly's too, as if some great thing were advancing from the clouds.

The grey girl tilted her head, obviously hearing something beyond the tumult of the ravens. Whatever it was, the sound of it shrank her back. She cast a panicked glance at Mup, pressed herself into the shadows of the vardo, and was gone.

Mup stepped out onto the porch. Dad and Emberly were racing across the roof garden now, a chaos of ravens around them. Some of the guard landed. They immediately rose up as warriors, their hands spread and aimed at the sky.

Silence fell down like a thunderclap. All movement ceased.

The airborne ravens, the running warriors, Emberly and Dad, all froze in their places.

The wooden porch creaked as Crow stepped to Mup's side.

Magda rose above the edge of the castle. There was ash in her hair, ash on her clothes, trailing her like a cloak. She stepped from the air into Crow's little garden. She was fierce and directed as a hawk, aiming straight for the two children who cowered like rabbits at the sight of her.

Mup went to summon lightning and realized, with horror, that none would come.

"You're sick," whispered Crow. "You've no energy left to use."

Magda strode through the cloud of ravens which she had suspended with her magic, past the motionless warriors. She passed Emberly and Dad as if they were no more than statues, creaked up the vardo steps, pushed Mup aside and snatched Crow.

"NO!" cried Mup, terrified Crow would burst to ash in Magda's hands.

Nothing happened.

Magda stared down at the boy dangling in her fist, as if astonished to see him still in one piece. She shook him. She grabbed his face between her hands.

"Leave him alone!" cried Mup.

Frustrated and confused, Magda tossed Crow from her.

He slammed into the bright wall of the porch and Mup grabbed him. "Are you OK, Crow?"

He nodded, rubbing his face where his mother's cruel grip had left bruises and ash marks in the shape of fingers.

"Did you do this to me?" hissed Magda.

"Do what?" snarled Crow. "Summon you? If I did, it wasn't what I meant to do. I was only thinking of you… I can't help it. I think of Dad, and when I think of Dad I can't help thinking of you and—"

"What are you babbling about? Summon *me*? No one summons me. I mean *this*!" She spread her ashy arms. "*This*!" She touched a budding blossom tree, it crumbled in her hands. "Why would you *curse* me like this?"

"I haven't cursed you!"

Magda stared keenly at him. "No," she said at last, "I don't think you have."

"Why did you touch him?" said Mup. "He could have turned to ash."

She expected one of Magda's clever, cutting answers. To her surprise the woman seemed to consider the question. "But he didn't," Magda muttered. "Why?" She paced for a moment, rubbing her hands together, then she shook off the topic. "Urgh, it doesn't matter." She pointed to Mup. "You're the reason I'm here, girl. I want you to fulfil the promise you made the night I rescued you from your grandmother's minions. I want you to help me."

"Help you? I can't fix this," cried Mup, pointing to the destroyed plant.

Magda pushed her terrible face close. There was dust on her skin, mingled with the ashes – the red and brown dust of the parched landscape she'd travelled since coming back to the borough. "I'm not asking you to fix it, you dreadful little scrap of nothing. Do you think I'm stupid? There is only one person strong enough to fix a curse like this."

"Mam's not here," snarled Mup. "And even if she was…"

"Pah!" spat Magda. "Your mam. She's nothing but a child, like yourself. An undisciplined, untutored wilderness dabbler. No, girl, I need a proper witch. Someone of power, who knows what she's doing." She grabbed Mup by her neck, swung her out from the porch and slammed her onto her knees. Grabbing Mup's hand she pressed it to the stones of the castle roof.

"Find your grandmother," she said.

"No one can find her!" choked Mup, struggling to

breathe. "Don't you think we've tried?"

"Try harder."

"Let her go!" yelled Crow, leaping onto his mother's back.

Magda elbowed him aside with no effort at all. He tumbled away.

Even as he rolled to his feet, Crow had begun to sing. Magda's hair rose from her shoulders as if underwater. Her clothes began to float. Her eyes widened as she realized Crow's voice was doing this to her. Mup, still pinned to the ground, felt Magda's weight lift from her as the witch rose into the air. Magda gasped with genuine fear.

Mup summoned what feeble sparks her weakened constitution could muster and stung Magda's choking hand. The witch only tightened her grip and pushed Mup harder into the stones. She turned her attention to her son. "Be still," she growled.

Crow froze. His voice fell silent. Magda's weight landed full force onto Mup again.

Then the witch surged to her feet. Dragging Mup with her, she walked around Crow as if he were a terrifying statue. His eyes were closed, his mouth opened on a powerful note, now silenced by his mother's sorcery.

"This is no ordinary clann magic," whispered Magda. "The boy's an actual ... he's an actual threat."

Within the vardo a sound made itself known. A tentative, searching noise, as if some huge wounded creature were hopelessly asking for aid. Magda's fierce attention turned to it.

Mup – dark spots dancing now – fought the witch's choking grip. Lightning fizzled at her desperately scrabbling fingers. "Mam will be back soon," she wheezed. "If you go now, she'll leave you alone."

"Stop your nonsense, child," murmured Magda, already dragging her up the vardo steps. She opened the vardo door. At the sight of the creature, she dropped Mup like a doll. Mup fell, gasping, to the floor. Magda stepped past her and went inside.

The creature lifted its head to her, seeking.

Magda went to touch its cheek, then withdrew her hand. "You," she whispered. "But how?" She looked back to where her son stood motionless in the last light, like the statue of a cockerel crowing, his head thrown back, his mouth open to the darkening sky. "Incredible," she said.

And then Magda was all action. Sweeping across Mup again, she touched a finger to Crow's forehead and he collapsed like a sack of grain. She threw him into the vardo.

Mup climbed to her hands and knees, still trying to

get her bruised windpipe to gasp in more than a trickle of air. Magda took her by the scruff of her neck, about to fling her off the porch. But then she stopped. She seemed to think. She let Mup drop again.

"I'll hold onto you," she muttered, rooting in her pockets. "Where's my … ah, here."

She withdrew a small glass pendant, dangling on the end of a bright chain. Mup's heart stammered at the sight of it. Magda huffed. "You've seen one of these before, have you? Well … here, get a closer look."

She shoved the necklace at Mup, spoke a rasping word.

There was a buzzing sound, and a crack of light: a noise like a kettle whistle. The air around Mup swirled like water spinning into a drain.

The world got very, very tiny then, and Mup was squashed inside it, like it was a frosted glass bowl. Everything swayed nauseatingly upwards. Mup saw Crow's garden from the strangest angle, all warped and far away. The world swung horribly, and then settled into a steady to-and-fro motion.

Mup realized that she was in the pendant, and Magda had slung it around her neck.

"Nooo!" she howled, battering the frosted glass.

There came a whistle, faint and distant. Magda was

calling up the tornado horses. Things swung in and out of view as Magda settled the tornados between the shafts, climbed onto the porch, and took in the steps. There was a distorted, distressing vision of Crow sprawled unconscious at the creature's dark feet, then Magda shut and locked the vardo's painted door.

She sat in the driver's seat. "Hup!" she said, slapping the reins down hard. "Hup!"

The vardo shuddered and took off.

Mup tried to shoot lighting. It died at her fingertips. She battered the glass.

"Dad!" she screamed. "Dad! Doctor Emberly!"

But Dad and Doctor Emberly were motionless in the dying light, the flock of raven guard suspended all around them. The vardo skimmed their heads, and then all Mup could see, when she pressed her face to the dull glass wall of her prison, was the rushing horses, the dark sky ahead of them, and the forest speeding by.

The Finder of Paths

Mup watched the light die and stars come out. Soon they were travelling through a brightly sparkling night sky. Were Dad and Emberly still standing out in the dark, the ravens frozen all around them? She hoped not. Mam should have been home hours ago – surely she would have freed them?

Mup listened for the boom and roar of Mam's rage: for signs that her mother had restored the palace, and was right that moment striding across the landscape, coming to her rescue. But the world was reduced to the cool orb in which she found herself imprisoned and there was no signal beyond her immediate surroundings.

It wasn't difficult to move inside her prison once she got used to it. Mup could feel her hands and feet and arms and legs – but it was as though she were made of smoke, twining around herself, filling the pendant, pressing against its interior surface. If she looked up, Mup could see a weird, warped version of what she supposed was Magda's chin, to the right and left the vardo's porch, and behind her, just darkness.

Mup twisted about, probing every inch of the glass, hoping to find a seam or a crack or a weakness through which she might slip. She closed her eyes. She pressed her palms to the surface. She thought, *Show me.* There was no reply, just the smooth deadness of glass.

She tried to call forth her hare shape... It didn't answer.

Magda chuckled. "It would be a poor cage that left its captive their powers, child."

Mup slapped the glass. She was smoke, that was all, powerless to do anything other than look and scowl. "Where are we going?" she yelled.

"No need to shout," murmured Magda. "I can hear you."

The witch was scanning the distance, watching for something. All of a sudden, she breathed gently outwards, as if finding what she sought. Mup followed her gaze. A thin glow silvered the horizon. It brightened, and Mup shrank back as the moon sailed, full and knowing, into the waiting sky.

Cold light illuminated the vardo, and Magda got to her feet. "See me, Majesty! See your repentant daughter!" She took the pendant from around her neck, and held it high. Mup found herself with nowhere to hide as the moon's great eye examined her through the milky glass. "I come bearing gifts of power and leverage," cried Magda. "Allow me bring them to you. Allow me find my way home to lay them at the feet of my powerful, merciful mother."

The moon sailed on, silent. Its light seemed to retreat as it climbed higher in the sky.

"Did she hear you?" whispered Mup.

Magda didn't answer. The world jolted again as she put the pendant back around her neck. Mup saw her hands tying the reins. She heard her murmur, "Steady," to the horses.

They went inside the vardo.

Mup pressed herself to the glass, straining to see as Magda lighted the lamps.

The witch faltered.

Crow, instead of being sprawled on the floor, was lying in the bed alcove, a blanket dragged across him. "Did you put him there?" she asked the creature.

The creature just continued to loom and moan, pressing himself to wall and bookshelf and ceiling, as if trying to feel his way into understanding. Magda raised her voice. "Make yourself useful," she told it, pointing to the open door. "Drive the vardo." It stumbled against a chair, almost bumping her and she drew back against the wall. "Careful," she whispered. "Don't touch me."

The pendant darkened as her hand closed around it, and Mup heard a muffled word.

There was a fizzing and a gasp of glitter. Mup popped out into the open air.

The creature loomed above her. Mup couldn't find her feet and she stumbled against it. Its flesh gave against her weight, a repulsive, marshy feeling. Mup recoiled, trying to hide her revulsion.

"Sorry," she said.

The creature seemed to notice her for the first time. It lowered its face to hers as if trying to see her.

"Hello," she whispered.

"Take him outside," said Magda. Still pressed to the wall, she had her hands held high, as if afraid she'd accidentally touch the creature.

She doesn't want to turn him into ash, thought Mup. But why? Magda hadn't cared about turning Crow into ash. And if this *was* Crow's dad, Magda was the one who had killed him in the first place – or so the queen had said. *Why is she being so careful about him?*

"Take him by the hand. Bring him outside. Give him the reins."

Mup did as she was bid.

The creature's hands were strong, yet somehow gentle. Mup could easily imagine him picking up Crow without hurting him, laying him tenderly onto his bed. He filled the porch with his bulk, huge and clumsy. But when Mup put the reins into his hands, he seemed to know what to do with them, and he settled down to driving the vardo as if finally finding something he could understand.

"He was always good with horses," murmured Magda. She had come up behind them in the porch. "A straight line, my love. That's all I need from you for now." Her hand hovered for a moment over the creature's dark hair, then she snatched Mup inside and shut the door.

"Sit there." She slammed Mup into a chair, and turned away.

Mup's hand crept to the table's surface, seeking a connection to the outside world.

Magda chuckled. "Do you think I'm a fool, girl? I've masked this vardo so deeply that not even you could find it, were you to stand right on top and drum your heels on the roof."

"Mam will find you," said Mup.

"Your mother can do nothing but shoot fire and tear down walls," murmured Magda, going to stand over Crow.

"Mam can do lots more than that!"

"Oh?" The witch cast her an amused glance. "What?" At Mup's silence, Magda turned back to her son. "Wake," she said.

Crow's eyes opened, wide and terrified.

"Climb down."

He climbed stiffly to the floor.

"Sit."

Crow sat across from Mup on the other side of the little fold-down table. His body was still and obedient, but Mup saw his bright eyes darting here and there as his mind tried to catch up.

"Your mam stole the vardo, Crow," she said very quickly. "The creature is driving it. She's taking us to the queen."

"Be quiet," murmured Magda.

Mup's words were stopped like a corked bottle. Magda leaned towards her son. His angry eyes switched from Mup to her.

"Crow, you are going to talk, but you are not going to sing. You will say enough to answer my questions and not a syllable more. Do you understand?"

"I understand."

"Who taught you to conjure the dead?"

Crow's eyes snapped wide with horror. "No one taught me to conjure the dead."

"You taught yourself?"

"No!"

Crow's face had reddened with rage. Mup could see there were many more words he wanted to add to these simple answers, but his mouth snapped shut at the end of each frustratingly brief reply. *Let him talk*, she thought. *Let him talk, you dreadful person.*

Magda regarded her son in silence for a moment. Then she went to the door, gazing through its stained-glass windows at the hulking figure on the porch. "You realize what you've done, don't you? You haven't just called forth a ghost here, boy. You haven't just resurrected the dead. You've *recreated* the dead – conjured a ghost from memory, assembled a body for it by will alone. You made a shambling job of it, but you did it none the less." She came and took her son's motionless hands. "Do you know how much you are worth to me?" she whispered.

"Far more than I was before, apparently!"

Crow's eyes shone at being able to score this point despite the terrible restriction on his words.

"Yes," said Magda, coldly dropping his hands. "Far more." She began to pace. "Wait until the queen hears this. A necromancer. A necromancer so powerful that he can call forth flesh from air – and still untutored yet. Still ours to mould."

Over my dead body! thought Mup. *Grandma's not getting her hands on Crow!*

"Speaking of the queen," muttered Magda.

She went to the porch. Mup instantly took Crow's hands. She squeezed down hard on Crow's flesh, feeling for the spell inside him, trying to break its hold, but it was like an iron cage around her friend, holding him in.

The vardo tilted. When Mup turned, she could see the tops of trees. They were spiralling downwards.

She ran around the table. *Come on, Crow. I'll fly us away.*

She tried to lift him. He was like stone in her arms.

Out on the porch, Magda murmured, "Land us there, my love."

A sly movement in the bookshelves drew Mup's eye. She shoved Crow aside, her hand up to protect him from who-knew-what. A face slid into view within the grain of the wood. It was the little grey girl. She put her ashy finger to her lips, then slid from sight as Magda's figure filled the door.

The witch huffed at the sparks dancing feebly on Mup's fingers. "You are your mother's daughter indeed. Did you hope to blast your way out? Fly your friend to safety? Rest assured, enchanted as he is, my son would have plummeted you like a stone. You're well used to that though, aren't you, Crow? Weighing people down."

Mup squeezed Crow's shoulder. *Don't let her get to you, Crow.*

Crow's fierce glare told Mup he wasn't.

It was very annoying not being able to speak. But there was something about having a friend there, about being able to look into Crow's eyes and know they had each other's companionship and support, that made things better.

Mup wasn't alone.

And neither was Crow.

Magda was.

Mup's feelings must have shown on her face, because Magda faltered – her expression uncertain. "What is happening?" She looked suspiciously around. "What are you up to?"

Mup lifted her chin in defiance. The vardo shuddered lightly as it came to land.

"Get out," growled Magda.

She shoved Mup, making her stumble. Crow jerked in his seat. The grey girl hissed in the shadows. Mup shook her head – *I'm OK* – and went outside.

The night was baking hot, the woods sere and crackling underfoot.

Magda looked around, as if seeing the countryside for

the first time. "What has your mother done to this place?"

Not Mam! thought Mup. *My grandmother! Your queen!*

Magda looked sidewsys at her. She sneered. "You're like a little stoppered flask, aren't you? With all those words choked up inside. How frustrating for you."

The vardo glowed in its own warm circle of lamplight. Magda stalked out of its radiance, pulling Mup with her. She walked until they were far into the trees. The moon was still bright, though far away now. Magda stood and stared up into its latticed light.

"Here, Majesty?" she asked.

Was it Mup's imagination, or did the moon glow a little brighter? Magda shoved her down into a puddle of its brilliance and it was icy, even on this sweltering night.

"Find me a path," hissed Magda.

Can I? thought Mup. After all her trying, and all her failures, was it possible the queen would just allow Mup to find her? She pressed her hands against the moonlit ground. They sparkled as if plunged into a pool of frost, and burned as if coated in ice.

Mup bared her teeth against the pain. *Show me,* she thought.

A single path crackled out from beneath her hands. Zigzagged and sharp, it cut like a scar of ice through the gentle earth, shooting eastwards. Mup followed it with her mind.

It was heading for a darkness that remained hidden just beyond Mup's reach, heading for a cloud of bitterness and spite. Heading for Grandmother. Heading for the queen.

Mup urged the path onwards. The place it led to was so horribly destructive and angry and dark. She didn't want to go there. Still she followed with her mind. Determined to know the queen's hiding place. Determined to find her grandmother at last!

The path stopped.

Mup held her breath. Wrist deep in agonizing cold, she waited for the path to continue.

But it didn't. Something – or someone – had blocked it.

"Speak," said Magda.

"She's only shown me part of the way."

"Then that is as far as we go."

Mup felt herself being snatched from the ground. Magda dragged her back to the vardo.

Mup didn't struggle. Even if she could have escaped – even if she *had* been willing to abandon Crow – there was no way she was leaving now.

Magda was bringing her to the queen.

She was bringing her to the queen!

Grandma was so close to being found.

Inside and Out

"Tell the horses," said Magda, dragging Mup to the vardo.

When it became obvious that Mup didn't know what to do, Magda shook her head.

"Haven't you ever told a storm which way to travel? Good grace, your aunt really was determined to waste you, wasn't she? Here!" She thrust Mup close to the swirling, gusty face of one of the horses. "Think of your route, then breathe the knowledge into the horse's nose."

The horse blinked stormy eyes at her. Mup leaned tentatively closer. It huffed a breath that smelled of pine forests in the rain. *What do I smell of?* wondered Mup. She hoped she smelled nice as she breathed gently into the horse's nostrils.

The horse sniffed curiously. Then it inhaled a full, deep, powerful breath.

Mup felt all the air being taken from her lungs, and

with it she felt a clear, bright certainty pass between them. The horse shook its cloudy head, and stamped its lightning foot, ready to go.

"Good," said Magda, and she pushed Mup up the steps and slammed the door, just as the vardo shivered to life.

Mup caught a brief glimpse of Crow, fuming at the table. Then Magda lifted the pendant, said the word and the world swirled up around her.

There was a surge of shadow just as Mup's world shut down. A dark thing streaked across the roof, and something leapt with her into the horrible confines of her glass prison.

Mup was afraid to move. She was afraid to speak in case Magda heard her voice.

There was definitely someone inside the pendant with her. She no longer fit smoothly like smoke against the sides. She could no longer twine gracefully around herself.

"Grey girl?" she whispered, pushing uncomfortably, trying to shoulder some room.

I am here.

The voice echoed inside Mup's mind. Not the grey girl's usual halting rusty voice, but a deeper, more powerful tone. Frightening.

"Are ... are you inside my head?"

Not exactly. We share the same space.

"It's very uncomfortable."

There was a rippling sensation, as if the grey girl had shrugged.

"Can you get me out of here?" whispered Mup.

In a way.

In a way? Mup wasn't sure she liked the sound of that.

Are you brave?

Mup was very tempted to say no. But she didn't really get the chance. She felt something like two arms snake around her. She heard the grey girl's rusty voice hiss in her ear, "Hold on." And she was pulled – *sploot* – like a cork from a bottle.

The little grey girl steadied Mup as she got her bearings.

A huge ceiling of stars sailed overhead. The ground was hard and curved. It thrummed slightly beneath her feet.

They were on top of the vardo!

"I can see through my legs!" cried Mup. "I can see through all of me!"

Realizing that she was yelling at the top of her voice, she clapped her hand over her mouth. Overhead, the stars continued to sparkle. The tornado horses continued rushing for the horizon. Beneath her feet the vardo shivered quietly as it journeyed through the air. No one came storming out onto the porch to see what the noise was.

"No one can hear you," rasped the grey girl. "No one sees you. You're a ghost."

"Am I dead?" asked Mup, whispering this time.

The grey girl shook her head.

"Where's my body?"

"Inside the pendant."

"I'm all grey. Why aren't I golden and sparkly like in the ghost place?"

"Your spirit did not break from your body, like it did in the ghost place. It is still attached. You feel the connection?"

Mup closed her eyes, she searched for a feeling of connection. "I feel it," she whispered. There was a sensation in her chest, as if an invisible thread was pulled tight there, a thread that stretched between Mup's heart and… Mup followed the thread with her mind. It stretched down into the vardo: down into the pendant that swayed at Magda's neck, inside which Mup's body lay curled like a nut in its shell, still breathing, still warm, still alive – but empty.

"I'm outside my body."

"Yessssss."

"My body is inside that tiny pendant."

"Yesssss."

"Oh, I don't feel good."

The grey girl caught her and lay her, light as thistledown, onto the roof of the vardo. Mup blinked up at the stars. She could feel Magda's enchantment down there, gripping her body in a painful vice. At the same time, she could feel her spirit-body, barely a spider's breath of weight, lying on the trembling roof of the vardo. Between them, the tenuous thread that held them together hummed like a guitar string.

"I can't imagine this is very good for me," she whispered.

The grey girl wagged her head. Agreement? Disagreement? Uncertainty?

Mup chose not to ask.

For the first time she noticed the strain on the girl's face. The dullness of her eyes.

"Are you sick, Girl?"

"Yes. Long way from home. I feel bad."

"I'm sorry. Thank you so much for staying to help me and Crow."

The girl's face pinched to that mask of hate so familiar to Mup.

"Minion hurts children," hissed the girl. "We will *stop* her."

"Yes," said Mup, struggling to sit. "Yes, we will."

She took the grey girl's hand, and they sat facing each other on the roof of the vardo, ghost to ghost under the stars. Mup thought deeply for a long time. The grey girl patiently waited.

"Can we fly when we're spirits, Girl? Can we travel?"

"Travel?" The grey girl frowned. "Like ... in the ghost place?"

"I don't know. Is that travelling? I meant more like could we—"

Before Mup could finish her question the grey girl tightened her grip on Mup's hands, flipped backwards off the roof and dived out of the world.

There was a sickening *shooting* sensation: the sense of the grey girl being pulled rapidly backwards through space. She had her arms clamped tight around Mup, and so Mup was carried with her.

They landed on their backs in pitch darkness.

Mup froze for a moment, a little terrified that she was all alone. Then the grey girl sat up beside her and their surroundings were illuminated by the faint glimmer of their combined ghost light. Mup felt the thread in her heart very clearly now – as if it had been stretched even tighter. It was an unpleasant, panicky feeling.

The grey girl's face loomed over hers. She was slightly more luminous than she had been in the vardo. Her face no longer as pinched and dull.

"You look a bit better," croaked Mup.

The girl's concerned expression implied that Mup, perhaps, looked worse.

Clutching her chest, Mup sat. "Where are we?" She peered around in the dim light. "The oubliette? Why would you bring me here?"

The girl shrugged. "Here is where I start," she said simply. "Here is where I always start."

"Well … OK. I need to find my mam and dad, though."

The girl looked up. Far overhead was a distant coin of illumination. Mup shuddered. Naomi had explained to her that this was one of the ways raggedy witches had punished people. They would lower them into the oubliette through a hole in the ceiling, and leave them there to die. That distant light must be the hole.

"Let's get out of here." With an enormous effort, Mup got to her feet, and flew towards the light. The grey girl slowly followed.

They emerged through the grating of a shored-up

drain and into a neglected garden.

Mup stumbled in the open air. It was very difficult to do anything at all. Mup honestly thought that without the grey girl's support, she would have just stopped moving.

"Feels like I'm wading through jelly," she gasped.

"You are a long way from your body," muttered the girl, gripping Mup's elbow. "Not good when you're still alive."

"Where are we?" asked Mup. "What is that dreadful noise?"

Supporting each other, the two girls followed the noise through a series of arches, down a series of corridors, into a warmly lit hall. Tipper was sitting at the bottom of some steps, howling his little doggy head off. Behind him, Marty and Grislet sat tear-stained and glum.

"Tipper!" gasped Mup, stumbling towards him. "Tipper, it's me!"

At the sight of Mup, Grislet rose to her feet. "Marty," she jabbered, pointing a shaking finger. "Marty ... look..." Her brother continued to stare sadly at his feet.

Tipper kept on howling. Mup and the grey girl had to cover their ears.

"TIPPER!" yelled Mup. "CAN YOU PLEASE STOP THAT RACKET!"

"I can't stop howling, Mup! I'm's sad 'cos you is deaaaaaad."

"We know," mumbled Marty. "You don't have to keep telling us."

"But, Marty…" stammered his little sister. "L-look…"

"I'm not dead, Tipper!" yelled Mup. "Can't you see me?"

"Of course I can see you, Muuuuup," howled Tipper. "You're standing right there!"

"What?" Marty's eyes snapped up. "Who are you talking to?" he asked Tipper. "Who are you pointing at?" he asked his little sister.

"It be the princess," said his sister, her face all aglow with wonder. "She be a ghost!"

"I don't have much time," gasped Mup, battling the increased pressure on her heart.

"How does she look?" asked Dad, peering sympathetically at the wall by Mup's head.

"Not good," murmured Doctor Emberly, lifting Mup's ghostly eyelid. "You've travelled too far from your body, my dear. It's not doing you any good at all."

"Then stop wasting time and let me talk to Mam and Dad!" gasped Mup.

"Of course." He moved aside.

Behind him, Mam's arms were crossed as tight as her frown. She was barely keeping herself in check. "Why can't we see her, Doctor?"

"Well, she's not actually a ghost, you see? She's more like a fetch, or a—"

"But we see *that one!*" cried Dad, gesturing to the grey girl.

"Ah, yes," said Emberly, eyeing the wary spectre. "Because she *is* a ghost ... I think. Actually, I'm not sure what she is. She might—"

"*Doctor!*" snapped Mam.

"Yes! Sorry! The point is, it appears our disembodied young hero is visible only to the very young, or to dogs."

"The point is," growled Mup, "I haven't much time and Crow is still stuck in that vardo with his dreadful mother."

"As are you, dear," Doctor Emberly gently reminded her. "You are only home in spirit, you know."

Black spots danced before Mup's eyes. She grabbed her chest, as the grey girl lowered her to the floor.

"She's after falling down!" cried Grislet.

"Tell Mam," Mup gasped to Emberly, "I don't know where Magda has us. Tell ... tell her I'm going to try find out. OK?"

"You need to go back now, my dear girl. Please. Before you do any damage."

112

Grislet pushed forward through the surrounding adults. She took Mup's ghostly hand. "Marty told Mam what he done," she whispered, her big golden eyes gazing down into Mup's fading ones. "He told her it weren't proper, to leave you struggling. He said he wouldn't have felt right down in his soul, had he let you turn to dust, and that he was glad he'd helped you in the end."

Mup looked past the small girl's face to where her brother flushed and scowled in the background.

"He also told our mam she should let me go to your school."

The pain in Mup's chest was very bad now. Everything was getting black around the edges.

"What... What did your mam say to that, Grislet?"

"She raged. And then she said alrightee. And then she cried ... but do you know, I think she was easier in herself after. I think... I dunno... I think it were like she felt right down in her soul."

"That's ... great ... I..."

There was a horrible fizzing feeling. Grislet's face filled with concern. The world doubled and trebled and blurred. Mup felt like someone was shaking her. "I'm going to throw up!" she yelled. And – pop! – she was inside the vardo, Magda staring at her in suspicion, the pendant in her hand.

Bravery

Mup blinked around her. The vardo was just as she'd left it.

Crow watched intensely from his motionless place by the table.

She smiled at him. His eyes smiled back.

"Where were you?" frowned Magda. "Why did it take you so long to materialize?"

"I was in there," said Mup, motioning to the pendant. "Where else would I have been?" She looked at Magda in surprise. "You've changed your clothes!"

"I've enchanted my clothes," muttered Magda.

"You look like *Clann'n Cheoil.*"

"Yes, well. I was *Clann'n Cheoil* for long enough. The horses wish to land. It must be the next step in the journey. I don't want to draw any more attention than necessary."

Crow's halting voice croaked from behind them.

"Your eyes will ... give you ... away."

Magda spun to him in amazement. "I gagged you! How can you talk?"

Crow glared triumphantly. "Going to have to ... work ... a bit harder ... Mam."

"Hush!" cried Magda.

Crow's mouth snapped painfully shut. But Magda had begun to look a little desperate, and his eyes shone with glee.

"Crow's right, you know," said Mup. "Your eyes are all black. Besides, won't people notice Crow's dad? He's hardly what you'd call inconspicuous."

"Fat lot you know," muttered Magda, and she flung open the vardo door and stalked outside.

Mup was astonished to find herself blinking in sharp morning sunshine. Only moments before she had been in the lamp-lit castle. Had time passed while she travelled between the two locations?

On the porch, Magda spoke quietly to the creature. "Good morning, my love."

Mup realized the witch had change his appearance too! He looked like nothing more alarming than a tall man, seated on the driver's bench of the vardo.

Is this what Crow's dad looked like? wondered Mup, coming out to look at him.

Yes. There could be no doubt of it. The man's dark eyes, his curling black hair, the sharp hawkishness of his handsome face: this was how Crow would look as a grown-up. This was Toraí Drummaker of Clann'n Cheoil.

But there was no hint of personality in Toraí's face. He was, as the creature had been, slack and slightly troubled, his entire attention focused on guiding the horses. A hot breeze lifted his long dark hair as he brought the vardo in to land. Warm scents closed around them: barbequed meat, fried dough and sugar, livestock. Mup realized with a start that they had landed at the edge of a market fair. The vardo wasn't even slightly out of the ordinary in this colourful, teeming place.

The waft of hot bread made Mup's stomach growl. "I'm starving."

"Don't even think about it," muttered Magda. "Just get out, find the path and get back in."

The woman was sweating and sleepless-looking, and Mup could see just how hard she was having to work in order to keep all the glamours going. Crow's dad's appearance; Magda's new disguise; the spell restraining Crow; the glamour that hid the vardo from Mam – all of them were starting to take their toll.

Crow chuckled. "Stretched ... a bit thin ... Mam?"

Something snapped in Magda. She spun and pointed

116

at her son. All the glamours shivered as the witch channelled everything into a single *zap* of magic. There was a *crack* and *squawk*, and instead of Crow sitting at the table there was now an iron cage and in it a raven, its beak bound with leather. "There," hissed Magda. "How do you like that?"

But Crow's eyes were triumphant over the gag. Realizing something was wrong, Magda straightened. She looked down at herself. "No," she whispered. "Why...?"

She was no longer dressed in the colourful clothes of *Chlann'n Cheoil*. She was no longer even dressed as an ordinary woman from the mundane world. She was, as she had always been under it all, a raggedy witch – stark and imposing and severe in black.

Magda seemed to notice the silence behind her. She turned. The bustling market crowd was frozen in shock, staring at the raggedy witch who had just appeared in the doorway of the recently landed vardo. Crow's dad was back to his misshapen self, a hulking creature by the witch's side.

"You lost concentration," said Mup. "They see you as you really are."

Magda stepped out onto the porch. The crowd contracted slightly, and she smiled a bitter smile. "That's right," she whispered. "You remember your place."

A tomato flew from nowhere and hit her in the face.

The crowd gasped. Some of them shrank back. Some of them turned away in fear. But Mup also saw people step forward. She saw people stand tall. And the more people who stood tall, the more others seemed to lose their fear. Magda – straightening slowly and wiping tomato juice from her cheek – saw the same. For the first time, Mup glimpsed uncertainty in the witch's face.

"Your kind isn't wanted any more!" shouted someone from the back of the crowd.

There was a rumbling of agreement. "Get out of here!"

Magda's face hardened. She allowed lightning to thread her fingertips. "Make me," she said.

By Mup's side the creature moaned. His troubled eyes pleadingly roamed the crowd.

Mup placed her hand on his bulky shoulder. "I'm scared for them, too," she whispered. Even as she spoke, she saw people in the crowd lift their hands in response to Magda's threat. She saw lightning and fire leap to their fingers.

Almost half the community stepped forward in defiance.

They're so brave, thought Mup, looking into the sea of determined faces. But these people had no idea who

Magda was. They had no idea how powerful she was. *Or maybe they just don't care any more. Maybe they just refuse to spend the rest of their lives bowing.*

Snarling, Magda raised her crackling hands.

Mup clawed her own hands. "Leave them alone, Magda."

The witch's black eyes dropped to the green fire which flared on Mup's fingertips. "What do you hope to do with that? Singe my eyebrows?"

"I don't know what I can do with it," said Mup. "And neither do you. But I do know that you can't fight us all – not without getting hurt anyway."

Magda sneered. She looked as though she were on the verge of no longer caring. She looked as though she might start shooting just out of tiredness and frustration. Mup let her own lightning die. "Don't hurt anyone, Magda. Just let me go out and find the queen's path. I'll get right back in, I promise. I won't cause you any trouble."

"Do it."

A man called out as Mup stepped down into the searing heat of the day. "Are you all right, little 'un? Do you need help?"

Mup crouched and pressed her hands to the mostly dead grass. "I'm OK."

119

"Come over to us," cried a woman. "We won't let that creature take ye."

Their kindness and courage almost made Mup want to cry.

You're so brave, she thought. *You're so, so brave.* "Where are we?" she asked.

Magda's voice came cold as ice from the porch at Mup's back. "Stop talking."

The man ignored her. "You're in *Cnoic na mBó Beag,*" he told Mup. "Near *Glas Gort.*"

"I don't know where that is. Can you get a message to my mam?"

Magda's command came again. "Stop *talking.*"

The man's eyes flicked to her in fear, but he stepped a little closer to Mup.

"Who is your mam?" he asked.

Who is my mam? What do I call her, when she refuses to be called "Queen"? "She's ... she's the old queen's daughter." The man's eyes widened. The magic that sparked at his fingertips faltered a moment in shock. "Tell her I was here, will you?" said Mup. "Send a message to the castle and—"

"STOP TALKING!"

Magda's lightning rent the air. People screamed and ran. Small fires flared where the lightning hit the

120

ground. Mup glared back at the witch. Magda seemed to fill the porch, her clothes and hair writhing, her face livid with anger. "Do. Your. Job!" she hissed.

Mup pressed her hands harder into the ground. The path opened up, and Mup's own rage propelled it on its way. The path cut like a sword slash past the fires Magda's lightning had started, past the crowd of people fighting those fires, out through the boundaries of the fairground and into the countryside. It ripped through miles of thirsty grassland, bisected oven-baked townships, divided the trees of suffering forests – and then stopped.

Mup saw the parched rocks of a shimmering mountainside. Near it she sensed the darkness again, that great roiling cloud towards which they were heading. She sat back. Such a huge, powerful bitterness lay there, waiting.

"Well?" asked Magda. "Where are we going?"

Mup took in the previously industrious marketplace. What she saw surprised her. The fairground was a shambles, smoke rising, flames flickering, and folks running about. But already people had the fires contained. Already, they were soothing their unhappy livestock. Soon they would have everything under control. Soon it would be as if Magda had never been here. *She's not in charge any more,* thought Mup. *Despite all the harm she could do to these people, she won't break them.*

"Where are we *going?*" insisted Magda.

Mup didn't answer. She went to the horses, stroked their velvet cloud-noses, breathed instructions into their lungs, and returned to the porch in silence. The creature that had been Crow's dad elbowed Magda aside as he took in the vardo steps. The witch lurched and had to steady herself as the horses took to the air.

In the receding crowd the man lifted his hand to Mup: *Be safe!*

Mup smiled at him: *Thank you.*

Magda watched this from her position against the porch rail. Mup thought she looked smaller, despite the damage she'd just caused. She looked confused. Mup had expected her to glower at the crowds until they were out of sight. Or to suck Mup up into the pendant as a show of power. Instead she stumbled into the vardo and shut the door.

Mup followed her.

Mam and Dad

Inside the vardo, Magda had come to a halt by the door, staring at Crow. He hopped from foot to foot in his cage, that angry glee brighter than ever in his round black eyes. The leather gag was lying on the table. Crow chattered his beak as if to demonstrate his freedom from it.

"How did you do that?" grated Magda.

Crow just laughed.

Magda went and stood over him, her clenched fists braced on the tabletop. "One note," she warned, "One single note out of you and I'll turn you into an earthworm."

"Pah," said Crow.

Mup glanced around the vardo. She was hoping to see the little grey girl. Magda had jerked her away from the castle so quickly that Mup had no idea if the girl had been able to follow. Her eyes fell on the gag lying limply on the table... How *had* Crow managed that?

She met her friend's gaze. He winked at her. "It's getting crowded in here," he croaked.

Mup grinned. The grey girl was here.

"How's my dad?" asked Crow.

"Your *dad*," huffed Magda. "What would you know of Toraí? You can't remember enough to even conjure him properly."

"I do so remember my dad."

"How could you? Your father was never home."

"That's not *true*."

"It is true, and you know it. Sealgaire raised you. Your *dad* was too busy to spare you anything more than an occasional visit."

"That's more than you ever gave me!" cried Crow.

Magda — seeing she'd finally needled past her son's cheery defiance — smiled. She turned from him in satisfaction, and began examining the shelves of the vardo. Her hand drifted over the many neat contents — the teacups, the pictures, the ornaments that Crow had retrieved or replaced since rebuilding his lovely home. Mup could see that the witch was regaining her control. Having someone to torment seemed to steady her.

"I'm sorry your mam is so cruel, Crow," said Mup.

"I'm not cruel," murmured Magda. "I'm honest."

"She's not honest," Mup told Crow. "She's mean. She's saying stuff just to hurt you."

"I know that," said Crow. "Dad loved me, and I loved him. Nothing she says will change that."

"Oh, do stop your prattling," said Magda.

"The only reason Dad wasn't home much was because he was fighting the queen. He wouldn't have had to do that if it wasn't for people like you."

Magda's mouth tightened.

"I'm proud of you, Crow," said Mup.

Crow blinked at her in surprise. "Thanks," he said. "I... I'm proud of myself!"

"Good. You and your dad should be proud. You both stand up to people that do wrong, even if they are stronger than you. Imagine if your mam had been like that."

Magda was getting that agitated look to her again. "Stop talking about me as if I weren't here," she snapped.

Mup ignored her. "Your mam is so powerful, Crow. She could make a real difference to this world if she used her magic for good."

Magda thrust her face up close to Mup's. "I do make a difference to this world," She was so close, her pale skin and black eyes so terrible, that Mup couldn't help but flinch. Magda sneered. "Couldn't keep ignoring me for long, could you, dear?"

Mup could make nothing out through the glass.

Was Magda lifting the cage? Was that her screaming?

"CROW!" yelled Mup. "CROW!"

She ... will ... hurt him.

"Grey girl?" Mup spun in her prison, trying to see. "Help him!"

Can ... not. Too ... weak.

The muffled noises from outside the orb were horrible – squawking and screaming.

Mup tried to grab the girl. She snatched only smoke. "Save Crow!" she cried. "Take him onto the roof like you did me!"

Too ... tired.

"We'll do it together!"

The girl paused, as if she hadn't ever considered the possibility. Mup grabbed again, hoping for a spectral hand. She found one. Together they leapt.

There was a bright flurry of chaos. Magda's snarling, shouting face. An iron cage being shaken in clenched white fists. Feathers flew. Mup and the grey girl swooped like hawks towards the centre of the cage. There was a surprised squawk, a momentary catch, and they were free and up, zooming through the roof of the vardo, a cloud of startled boy-shape dangling from their arms.

* * *

"Let me go!" yelled Crow, kicking and struggling in a frenzy of panic. "Let me go, you rotten hag!"

"Crow, it's us!" yelled Mup.

"You'll be sorry! Wait and see. I'll sing the flesh off your bones! I'll sing your eyeballs inside out! I'll—" Crow came to a startled pause, clinging to the roof of the vardo. "What?" he said. He looked around, taking in the open sky: the breeze that ruffled his hair, the half-amused, half-distraught face of his best friend. "Mup ... where?"

Then he saw the grey girl and the shock sent him sliding down the curved side of the roof.

Mup dived and grabbed him, and for a moment he was dangling over the edge, staring up into her face. "You're ... you're see-through," he said. He looked down at their transparent hands, gripping tightly onto one another. "We're both see-through!" he yelled, as Mup heaved him over the edge. "We're ghosts! Mam's killed us, Mup! She's killed us! Who'll stop her now?"

"We're not dead, Crow! You're still connected to your body! Can't you feel it?"

Crow calmed. He put his transparent hand to his transparent chest. Mup saw the moment when he found the invisible thread that hummed between his ghost-heart and his body in the vardo below.

129

"Can you feel it?"

Crow nodded. "I thought Mam had killed me," he whispered. "She was so angry."

"It's my fault, Crow. I wanted her to know how unimportant she was ... so I ignored her. It made her very angry. She took it out on you."

"It's what people like her do," rasped the grey girl wearily. "They hurt people who can't fight back, just to make themselves feel big."

Crow looked down at the vardo. "It's gone very quiet down there. What do you suppose she's up to?"

Mup pressed her ear to the roof.

"What you doing?" frowned the grey girl.

"Trying to hear what's going on," whispered Mup.

The grey girl looked at her as if she was quite spectacularly stupid. "You're a *ghost*," she said. "Ghosts don't have to listen. Ghosts can *look*." And she stuck her head down through the roof of the vardo, like plunging it into a pool of water.

How marvellous, thought Mup, and she did the same.

Mup had to giggle when she realized that she and the girl were hanging upside down, two disembodied heads poking through the roof of the vardo. *All Crow will see is our bums sticking up in the air.* But then she followed the girl's bleak gaze to the table below, and her amusement fled.

Crow's body was lying in a drift of feathers at the bottom of the battered cage. His eyes were closed. His beak slightly open. His feet curled loosely into his chest. He looked dead. He looked well and truly dead.

Magda was sitting heavily in one of the vardo's little painted chairs, staring at him.

"I didn't mean it," she told his motionless body. "Wake up."

Mup yanked her head back into the open air. Crow was sitting on his haunches, waiting expectantly. At the look on Mup's face, his expression fell. "Crow," she said, "don't take this the wrong way, but ... are you sure you're not dead?"

"It's hard not to take that the wrong way, Mup!"

"Boy is not dead yet," rasped the grey girl.

"I'm not sure I like how you said yet," muttered Crow.

The grey girl shrugged. Mup supposed being dead wasn't something a ghost would consider overly serious. She went to speak, but Crow held up a hand as if to prevent her telling him anything more.

"Whatever my mother has done to me,

Crow definitely wishes not to see."

With a sigh, the grey girl lay down on the roof of the porch. Her light was getting very dim.

"Is she all right?" asked Crow. "She looks even deader than usual."

"You should go home, Girl," said Mup.

"Without me, children will not be able to jump from bodies; children will not be able to travel. I stay."

Mup knelt at the girl's side. To her immense surprise, the girl pressed in close against her. Mup gently stroked her ashy back. The girl curled up like a big strange cat, and shut her eyes.

Mup anxiously scanned the landscape that whizzed by below. Great grass plains, burned dry by the merciless sun, stretched as far as the eye could see. Up ahead there was no sign of any mountains. But Mup knew they were there, growing closer every moment.

Grandma was just over the horizon.

"What's the plan?" asked Crow.

"Find the old queen."

"And then?"

Mup felt a blaze of fierceness. "Make her *stop*. Make her admit that her time is over."

"You're bringing my mam to her. You know that, right? One of the strongest witches in the borough – the queen's main enforcer – and you're bringing her right back to the queen's side."

"People threw *tomatoes* at Magda, Crow. The raggedy

witches aren't as strong as she remembers. The people may not be as powerful as the witches, but they've reclaimed their magic, and they'll never let themselves be pushed around again."

"Hmm," said Crow. He lowered himself over the edge of the porch roof. "I'd be a touch more confident if the person saying that wasn't currently trapped in a pendant around my mother's neck." He swung in beneath the overhang, and disappeared from Mup's sight.

After a moment, his voice – odd now, and ghostly, but still achingly sweet – drifted up in song.

"Boy is singing again," murmured the grey girl. "Sound's nice, now he's not so alive."

Not so alive? thought Mup. *I don't like the sound of that.*

She lay on her stomach and peered anxiously over the edge.

Crow was sitting close to the creature on the driver's seat, singing to himself as he watched the fields stream by. At first, the creature drove the horses onwards as always, its face creased with the usual confusion and distress, but as Crow's song continued, Mup saw the tension leave the creature's misshapen body. She saw the dark brow clear.

The creature turned its eyes to the small luminous boy sitting by its side.

Sensing his gaze, Crow looked up. "Hey, Dad," he whispered.

The creature lifted his arm. Crow slipped beneath it and leaned against the creature's side. The creature closed his arm around him, and Crow went back to singing.

Mup looked from him to the little grey girl, lying dark and silent at her side. Her two fierce, defiant friends. They had already suffered too much. Things were only going to get worse for them.

Mup set her jaw. She got to her feet.

The girl blearily raised her head. "Where are you going?"

"I'm taking you home," said Mup, and she grabbed the little girl and leapt off the side of the world.

The Grey Girl's Path

The grey girl's howl followed them into the corridors of the dead. Mup could feel the castle out there somewhere, trying to pull the girl home. But the girl fought against it. Wailing miserably in Mup's arms, she clung to the foggy walls, slowing their progress.

"You left Boy alone. You left him alone with that minion."

As the girl spoke, the pull of the castle dragged her slowly along the floor of the corridor. At the same time, Mup could feel the thread in her own heart trying to pull her in the opposite direction — back towards her body. She began to understand how this travelling thing worked. They were like two elastic bands, she and the girl, tied together and stretched between distances. The grey girl was being pulled towards the castle, Mup was being pulled towards the vardo. *If I let go of her, she'll just* zip back to the castle. She'll be safe – she'll get better. And I'll zip back into my own body and ... and I'd have one less person to worry about.

"You need to go home," she whispered into the girl's ear. "You're getting sicker and sicker all the time, and I'm worried for you."

The girl scrabbled desperately at the walls, her fingers raising clouds of fog as she fought to return to the vardo. "Please do not make me go,' she gasped. "Children need me. I'm ... helping them. I'm ... helping..."

Abruptly the girl went limp, and Mup realized that they were no longer being dragged towards the castle. They had stopped.

The girl turned very dark in Mup's arms.

"Girl?" Mup shook her. "Girl?" Clouds of ash began to rise from the small, still figure. The huge eyes were closed. She seemed entirely unconscious.

Mup tightened her grip as the tug on her heart began to pull the girl and herself back towards the vardo. Clouds rose in trails as they shot backwards – away from the castle, away from where the girl needed to be.

"NO!" yelled Mup.

She dug her heels in and they stopped.

With considerable effort, she rose to her feet. The grey girl was nothing but a feather weight in her arms, now. Nothing but an ashy cloud. Mup leaned forwards against the pull on her heart. She forced herself to take one step, then another, away from the vardo. She could have been heading anywhere: there were no maps to guide her in this grey and featureless world, no network to open up. But Mup was determined to find a path. She would find the grey girl's path. And she would bring the girl home.

And suddenly she was plummeting downwards.

The grey girl fell from her arms.

All was darkness and cold, and Mup hit the ground with a thump and a rattle of dry bones.

She lay breathless for a moment, her hand clenched tight over the tension in her heart. Then she pushed to her knees. "Girl?" she whispered, feeling about in the shifting debris of what she realized was the oubliette. Her ghostly form shed hardly any light down here, and nothing at all came of rubbing her fingertips together. "I really do not like being a ghost," she muttered.

Then − ah! − her hands closed on something colder and softer than the dryly rattling bones. There was a faint shimmer as her ghost-flesh met the girl's. "Are you...?" Mup had been about to ask, "Are you alive?" but that wasn't right at all. She gathered the girl to her, looked up to the dim coin of light above and launched painfully into the air.

* * *

"Doctor Emberly! Doctor EMBERLY!"

Mup squeezed up through the drain and out into a blast of sunshine. The grey girl hung in her arms like an ashy rag. Mup laboured up steps and into interior corridors, howling for help. Two members of Chlann'n Cheoil came towards her, frowning and speaking tiredly to each other.

Almost crying with relief, Mup held the girl out to them. "Help! Get the doctor!"

The couple passed through her without even a moment's hesitation.

Mup gasped and froze. Her eyes and ears filled with living colours, with the rush of breathing, with the murmur of voices. Then the couple walked on.

Mup gagged, breathless for a moment, then she straightened and howled, "DOCTOR EMBERLY! I NEED YOU!"

Her voice died away in ghostly echoes, inaudible to the living ear.

No one answered, and she stumbled on.

Sunshine and laughter filtered through from a door ahead and Mup staggered towards it, not heeding where she was. She came into the classroom. The stained-glass windows splashed her with colour as she carried the girl through their reflections.

"Dad!" she yelled. "DAD!"

She could see him sitting outside, surrounded by older children. The children all had their hands pressed to the ground, and they and Dad were listening intently as Marty murmured to them.

No one heard Mup, even though she was shouting at the top of her voice.

No one saw her as she carried the girl towards the door.

Marty slowly lifted his hand from the earth and a soft, bright bubble of water rose beneath his palm. The others, frowning in concentration, did the same. Brightness shivered beneath each hand as every child drew forth a gleam of moisture from the parched ground. There were shouts of triumph. Dad yelled something encouraging.

Mup stumbled from the classroom and out into the garden. Overhead, a tracery of silver mist kept off the harsh sun. The air was blessedly cool. Green shoots were beginning to show in the flowerbeds. The trees had begun to push forth new leaves.

Mup staggered through this newborn loveliness without anyone seeing her.

At the far end of the garden, members of the clann were singing the mist into being. With them a choir of tiny children harmonized their own threads to the magic. Mup lurched towards them. The very small children were the ones to see her at last. At last, they heard her ghostly cries.

The choir broke up in shrieks and screams.

Do I look that terrible? Mup thought, shocked even through her misery at the violence of the children's reactions. Then she caught sight of herself in one of the big windows and she could not blame the tiny children for their fear. She was hollow-eyed and dreadful: a shambling spectre, carrying something even more dreadful in her arms, and offering it to any who would take it. Goodness knows how her voice sounded to these very small people. Awful, probably. Awful, because Mup felt awful. She felt terrified and angry and despairing, and perhaps that's how her voice made others feel too.

Truly I am a ghost, she thought. *Truly this is how a ghost must feel. Alone and desperate with no one to hear them except those that run away in fear.*

And then there was a kind face looking down into hers, and gentle hands pried the poor girl from her arms, and Mup croaked, "Help her, Doctor Emberly. Help her. I think she's dying." And Naomi took Mup in her ghostly embrace as Doctor Emberly lowered the grey girl to the flagstones, and Dad and Fírinne were calming the children, and Mup was able to stop for just one moment, because she was back with people who cared enough to pause, who cared enough to listen, who cared enough to look past their own fear and see a desperate child who needed their help.

"Is she dead, Doctor Emberly? I mean, is she...? Is she...?"

"I know what you mean, princess," murmured Doctor Emberly, leaning over the grey girl's dull figure. She was nothing but a shadow on the flagstones. Mup could barely make out her features. "Oh, you poor thing," said the doctor. "You really have tried too hard, haven't you?"

To Mup's astonishment, the grey girl's eyes opened. She looked up into Doctor Emberly's face. "Erassssmussss," she breathed.

"Yes, my dear friend. Yes. It is I."

The girl tried to rise. It was a painful, distressing movement. Mup's eyes filled with tears just watching her. "Minion has the children. Must help. Must..."

"Shhhh," soothed Emberly. "Please don't exert yourself any further."

Gasping, the girl clung to him. "Must help. Can't leave them."

Emberly gently restrained her feeble struggles. "My dear friend, you are strong and you are brave. But look around you. Look..." He directed the girl's attention to the ring of young and old now gathered about them. "These people are here to help. You no longer have to do battle alone."

The girl gazed in astonishment at the sympathetic faces. Gradually she subsided into Emberly's arms. "They will … help?"

"Yes."

Her eyes, still roaming in amazement from face to face, drifted shut. She was fading fast.

"She is almost out of time," said Naomi.

"We need to lay her with her bones," Emberly told Mup. "But … does she even *have* bones? I've never been too sure of what the girl is. Did she ever have a body?"

"Are you talking to Mup?" whispered Dad, hunkering down beside him. "Is she here?"

"Hi, Dad," whispered Mup. Dad didn't hear her.

Naomi helped Mup to sit. It was strange to look into the witch's usually severe face and see nothing but undisguised concern. It was strange, and nice, to find herself lovingly supported by her. "We need to find this poor creature's resting place, Mup. It is our only hope of saving her."

"She starts off in the oubliette. That's what she told me. She always starts in the oubliette."

Naomi exchanged a glance with Doctor Emberly. "It is worth a try, Erasmus."

The doctor nodded. He went to rise. "I shall convey her there."

142

"Doctor," said Mup, holding him in place. "Crow is hurt too."

"What do you mean, Crow is hurt? How is he hurt?"

"What's going *on*?" insisted Dad. "*Tell me*. Is Mup here?"

"She is here, sir," Naomi assured him. "I have her right here by my side."

"Is..." Dad made a gentle gesture in the air near Mup. "Is she all right?"

"Her time as a ghost is taking its toll."

Mup gripped Emberly's jacket. She could feel the pull on her heart growing stronger. Soon she would have to leave. "Crow's mam hurt him, Doctor Emberly. I need you to come back with me. I need you to check if he's OK."

Emberly looked desperately from Mup to the girl fading rapidly in his arms, obviously torn between them both.

Naomi rose decisively to her feet. "I will take the grey girl."

"Oh, my dear, I cannot allow it. You know the girl's history with the queen's enforcers. The grey girl is not a child. She is a very powerful entity. Should she come to full strength and wake to find herself alone with you... Well, she could do you immense damage."

Naomi stooped and lifted the girl from his reluctant arms. "I will take care of this one," she insisted. "You help the others." She carried the girl away in a swirl

143

of dark cloak, passing through the yielding wall of the castle as if she were a stone dropped into a well.

Mup tugged Emberly's hands to bring his attention back from where Naomi had disappeared. "Doctor, where is my mam?"

"She... She and the raven guard are hunting for you, my dear. She received word that you were near *Glas Gort*, and she—"

"We were!" cried Mup. "We've moved on now, though. We're travelling over a big grass plain ... we're heading for mountains. "Oh!" she gasped, clutching her chest. "Oh... I don't feel right."

The doctor gripped her hand. "You must return to your body now, dear. It's not good for—"

"I'm going to try leaving signs for them to follow," she gasped. "Tell Dad! Quickly!"

Doctor Emberly urgently repeated her message.

Dad groaned in frustration and anguish. "But is she—?"

The rest of his words were lost as Mup shot backwards through space, Doctor Emberly's hand still gripped tightly within her own.

A Royal Offer

This must be what a ping-pong ball feels like, thought Mup, as she sped backwards through foggy corridors.

Doctor Emberly trailed behind, his hands clamped firmly in hers, his ruffled collar flapping like a paper plate, his eyes wide, his mouth a perfect roundness of surprise.

I must be careful not to land back in my body, thought Mup, *or we both might end up trapped in Magda's pendant.* She shut her eyes. She concentrated very, very hard. *I want to land on the roof*, she thought. *I want to land on the roof. I want...*

BANG! *Rumble, rumble, rumble.*

They bumped, then rolled, then fell into hot, buffeting air.

It was night-time again, the sky a vast umbrella of twinkling stars.

Mup found herself gazing up at the underside of the vardo as she and Emberly tumbled towards the ground.

"Quick!" she shouted, and they shot up and after the rapidly receding wagon.

Emberly got there first, He grabbed the carved good's rack, and reached for Mup. For a moment they trailed hand in hand behind the vardo, like a faintly luminous flag, then Emberly flipped Mup onto the roof, and scrambled after her.

"Oh, my!" he gasped. "That was exhilarating! I haven't felt so alive since... Well, since I was alive!"

But Mup's attention was on the horizon. She went to the edge of the roof, staring at the mountains which now loomed, dark and ominous, on the far side of the vast grasslands.

"We're nearly there," she whispered.

Crow stuck his head above the porch. "Mup! Where have you been? Do you see what we're heading for? Oh, hello, Doctor!" He scrambled up onto the roof. "Look, Mup!" He pointed to the distant mountains. "The queen's there, isn't she? I can feel it."

"Yes," said Mup, still gazing at the mountains. "She's there."

"My dear boy," cried Doctor Emberly, obviously alarmed at Crow's disembodied state. "Have I arrived too late? Please tell me you have not expired!"

"What? Stop it, Doc!" Crow brushed Emberly's

attempted examination aside, and grabbed Mup. "What are we going to do?"

"I don't know," whispered Mup, awed by the sheer darkness of what lay ahead.

"But, my boy," insisted Emberly. "Do you have any pain? If you close your eyes, can you tell me which parts of your living body might be injured? It's terribly difficult to examine the incorporeal self, you see. One does so need the body..."

"Doc!" snapped Crow. "I'm not what's important right now!"

"Not true," breathed Emberly, dropping to his knees before the impatient boy. "Not true. We are all of us important. No matter what events are happening. No individual's well-being should ever be overshadowed by the history that surrounds them."

Crow's face softened at the doctor's obvious concern. Before he could reply, the porch door slammed open below. They all shrank back as golden lamplight illuminated the striving horses. Magda's weary voice rasped, "Take us down, my love."

The creature slapped the reins and gave a low whistle. The horses began to spiral down. Mup signalled silently to her companions, and sank through the roof into the vardo below.

* * *

Magda was standing in the porch, staring at the mountains ahead. As the three friends drifted to the floor, the witch shut the door, blocking her from their sight.

"Will she be able to see you if she comes in?" whispered Mup to Emberly.

"Not unless I wish it."

"Are you sure? Magda's very powerful."

"No point worrying over what we can't control, my dear. Let's just…" He bent over Crow's bird-body lying in its drift of feathers at the bottom of the buckled cage.

Crow looked away as the doctor prodded the raven's curled foot. "That's just too weird," he muttered.

"Can you feel anything?" asked Emberly.

"A little tingle, that's all."

Outside, Magda murmured. The vardo juddered as it touched the ground. *Why is she stopping?* wondered Mup anxiously. *The queen's path took us all the way to the mountains — why would Magda want to delay?* "Hurry up, will you, Doctor?"

"It's just so difficult," murmured Emberly, examining the limp bird through the bars of the cage, "when the spirit is no longer inside the body." He looked sympathetically at Crow. "I don't suppose I could prevail upon you to temporarily re-enter?"

148

Crow's cranky impatience dissolved. "I'm afraid," he whispered. "What if it hurts?"

"Oh, Crow," said Mup. He allowed her to take his hand.

I hate your mother, she thought. *I hate her so much.*

"Just try for a moment," urged Emberly gently. "Just so I can ascertain…"

Crow shut his eyes. There was a soft, whooshing noise, like the sound a candle might make if one could hear a candle snuff out, and Mup's fingers closed on empty air. Crow had disappeared. The raven at the bottom of the cage stirred and croaked. It feebly moved its legs. Doctor Emberly bent over it.

The door opened, startling them both. Magda swept in. She looked terrible – grim and sleepless and angry. She strode towards the table with no indication that she saw them, but still Mup and Emberly drew back. Crow was moving weakly, his beak opening and closing, his feet grasping empty air. When Magda saw this, her eyes widened and she snatched the cage, staring in through the bars. "You're alive," she hissed. "Thank grace."

She cares, thought Mup, startled at the tears in the witch's eyes, astonished at the gentle way Magda placed the cage back on the table. *She's cared about him all along.*

But this foolish thought was shattered at Magda's next words.

"You're not to die, do you hear me? I need to give you to the queen." She slumped into the chair, and stared fretfully out the door at Crow's creature. "A necromancer," she muttered. "There's no way she'll reject me if I bring her a necromancer. And such a powerful one too." She glared at her son. "Get better. Quickly. The queen's moon will rise soon. She'll be looking for me. I don't want her to think you're irredeemably broken."

"What a dreadful woman," snapped Doctor Emberly. He stalked back to the table and leaned over the cage. "Can you hear me, dear boy? Just click your beak if anything hurts." He began moving his shimmering fingers through the raven's trembling body. "I'll be as quick as I can," he murmured. "Stay with me now..."

Mup walked right up to Magda, and leaned down, staring into the woman's pale, frowning face. "I don't like you," she whispered. "You're cruel and you're selfish and you've wasted everything good about your life."

Magda continued to stare right through her, her eyes restlessly roaming the glistening grasslands beyond the vardo door.

"You're all alone," whispered Mup. "No one cares for you, because you've never given anyone a reason to care."

Magda's troubled brow creased even further. "All alone," she whispered.

"Yes!" whispered Mup. "Crow's not alone. No matter what you tell him. He has people who care about him. He has friends who look after him. Because he's a good person, Magda, because he's a good person who cares what happens to others. Not like you."

Magda shook her head in self-pity. Tears rolled slowly down her face.

"You sold your family and friends to keep yourself safe. You hurt other people because the queen told you to. And for what? You have nothing now."

"I have nothing."

A silvery light was growing behind Mup. It spread a shimmering illumination into the vardo, cancelling the lamplight, and winking in cold highlights from delph and metal and glass as it pushed its way into the interior. Mup turned to see its source. The queen's moon had risen from behind the black mountains. Mup stared defiantly into its great stupid face.

"The queen is defeated, Magda. She'll never rule this kingdom again. You're too afraid to even face her without sacrificing your son. But the rest of the kingdom has turned its back on her. No matter what she does, she's lost. And there's nothing you can do about that."

Mup turned as she said this, smiling triumphantly into Magda's face. Magda was all illuminated with moonlight now, her tears glittering like frost in its chilly light.

Her black eyes stared straight into Mup's.

"Well, hello there," she hissed, grabbing Mup by the arm. "Who let you out of your little cage?"

Mup looked down at herself in alarm. The light had filled her with swirling glitter and dense milky fluorescence. She was brilliantly, almost vengefully, visible.

She shot Doctor Emberly a glance, he was pressed against the wall, safe in the shadows, staring wide-eyed at the moonlight which brushed only the toes of his buckled shoes.

Magda spun Mup to face the door, thrusting her into full view of the sailing moon. "I am not alone," she hissed. "I am not alone and I am not forgotten." Her breath was hot in Mup's ear. The moon was full and blinding in Mup's eyes. "My queen waits for me. She, and all my brothers and sisters. Soon we shall unite. Soon we shall march. And when we do, those fools who have dared to spit at me – those who dare to howl vengeance – they will be the first to suffer."

Magda rose over Mup, her hair and clothes writhing with feverish triumph. "Will I show you who is alone, little ghost? Little nothing." Magda gripped the pendant around her neck and shook it so that the world around

Mup rattled. Mup cried out. Magda laughed. "Cross me again and I'll crush this necklace like a bug. Then see what becomes of you."

Enraged, Emberly leapt from the shadows. The moonlight glittered on his arm as he reached to snatch the pendant from Magda's fist.

Get back! thought Mup. *She'll see you!*

But, before this could happen, Magda dropped the pendant. She cast Mup aside, and strode eagerly to the vardo door, staring up at the lowering moon.

Free of the witch's grasp. Mup threw herself into the doctor's arms. They tumbled into the shadows; out of the reach of the treacherous moonlight. Doctor Emberly was safely invisible once more.

He glared furiously at Magda. Mup whispered, "Calm down."

Magda paid no heed to either of them. She was gazing up at the moon with a lunatic fervour.

"I am here, Majesty," she called. "Your faithful daughter is here."

The moonlight pushed past her – Mup saw it actually shove Magda aside as it poured its way into the vardo. The witch watched, open-mouthed, as the light flowed across the floor and up the legs of the table, oozing its way over to where Crow lay blinking in his battered cage.

Glistening tentacles caressed the crooked bars. Frosty light illuminated Crow's glossy feathers.

Crow stared up at the great pale face that hung outside his door. For a moment, he seemed to listen to a voice no one else could hear. Then he croaked a laugh.

"Dream on, Queenie. I'd rather die than work for you."

There was a faint shivering in the air. The feel, but not the sound, of cruel, icy laughter.

Then the moonlight flowed across the table to Mup.

Mup stepped forward to meet it. "Hello, Grandma," she said.

The moonlight touched her and she felt the dry, cold voice of her grandmother form words in her head. *Hello, granddaughter. Aren't you in a pickle?*

"I'm not the one hiding up the mountains throwing tantrums with the weather, while the world gets on without me."

There was a moment of pause – as if the moonlight were taken aback – then the sensation of laughter came again: harsher this time, a touch forced. *Big words for someone as trapped and helpless as you are.*

Mup shook her head in disgust. "Of course I'm trapped," she said. "Of course I'm helpless. I'm small. I'm alone. And you're a powerful witch. It's always going to be easy for you to hurt me… That doesn't mean you're right. It doesn't mean you've won. It just means you're a bully."

Magda listened with undisguised dismay. "The queen is speaking to you?" she whispered. "What is she saying?"

Mup ignored her.

Moonlight twined itself in glittering ropes around Mup's waist: crawled up to breathe ice onto her cheek. *We agree on one thing*, it said. *You are small. You are alone. Magda could do anything she wants to you… But I can protect you from her. I can help you. Would you like to become the most powerful witch in the Glittering Land? I could do that for you. Just speak to your mother, convince her to work with me, and all my power will be yours.*

"My mother will never work with you."

"Your mother?" cried Magda in alarm. "What is the queen offering your mother?"

"Nothing but lies," snarled Mup. She turned again to the moonlight. "I might be small, Grandma, and I might be alone. But that doesn't change the fact that you've lost. The people have learned to work together now, and that makes them stronger than you can ever be. They'll never bow to you again."

From his cage, Crow croaked a mocking rhyme.

"*The time has come to say begone,*
To all the evil you brought on,

155

No more hatred growing here,
No more people bent in fear
Wild magic, free and strong,
Is the rule from now on."

The moonlight shuddered – whether from rage or something else entirely, Mup couldn't tell – and began to withdraw its frosty light.

"What of me, Majesty?" cried Magda. "Have you no words for me?"

The moonlight flowed around her as it drained from the vardo. Magda ran after it. Out onto the porch she ran, down the vardo steps, and far out on the grassy plain, lifting from the ground as she did so. But no matter how high she flew, the moon rose higher still, shrinking and retreating, until it was just a coin of distant light far beyond her reach.

Eventually, Magda's arms fell to her side, and she drifted back to earth. Her long black shadow came up to meet her as she hit the ground.

She stood out there a long time, cold and alone, her face turned towards the heedless sky as the moon sailed on without her.

Mutual Disapproval

"Magda's coming back, Doctor Emberly," said Mup, eyeing the witch as she tramped across the moonlit plain.

The ghost glanced up. His hands were inside the cage, wrapping Crow's dislocated wing against his body.

Crow glared between the bars at his approaching mother. "I could sing the flesh from her bones," he muttered.

"Please don't, Crow."

His fierce eyes met Mup's. "Why not?"

"Quite aside from how disgusting that would be? If the queen thinks we're helpless, she might allow Magda bring us to her. If she thinks we're ... we're..."

"Capable of singing the flesh from her bones?" suggested Emberly.

Mup shuddered. "Well, yes. If she thinks we're

157

capable of that, she might disappear in a puff of smoke and we'll never find her."

Crow huffed his agreement.

Emberly glanced out of the door. Magda was closer now. Her hair crackled with angry lightning. Each furious step sent up sparks.

"You need to make yourself invisible, Doctor," warned Mup. "She's in a terrible mood."

The doctor just went back to his task, his face grim, his hands gentle as he knotted the strips of silk scarf that he'd torn up as bandages. "Let her see me."

"But, Doctor!" gasped Crow.

"Let her see me."

"She's almost here!" cried Mup.

Crow flopped back down onto the floor of his cage. His eyes went glassy. He allowed his head to loll. Mup was very impressed at how ill her friend could make himself appear. She felt the hairs rise on her arms as Magda stalked up the steps. The air in the vardo fizzed with static electricity. The witch brought thunder into the room.

Startled, Magda froze in the doorway, her black eyes fixed on Doctor Emberly.

"Who are you?"

Emberly straightened. "Just a person, madam. Small and alone, doing my best."

"Did Crow conjure you?"

Her son moaned weakly, and Magda stepped forward to frown at him. "Hah," she breathed. "He is injured, and so he conjured a doctor." She touched the bars of the cage. "Truly he is his mother's son. Who would have known it?" She glared at Emberly. "Make him whole again. Or I'll cage you in lightning for the rest of eternity."

"You do not have to threaten me, madam! It is my honour and my duty to heal the sick."

"Oh, do shut up." Magda glared about the vardo. "Where's the other one, the heir's child? Still creeping about as a ghost? Plotting and sneering behind my back. Well, no longer."

Magda grabbed the pendant and spat a word.

There was a horrible slamming sensation. Mup's body and spirit reunited in a flash of glitter. The vardo spun. Mup staggered. She had been too long as a ghost. Her flesh felt heavy as a suit of armour. Her legs couldn't hold her weight. She crashed to the floor.

Doctor Emberly fell to his knees at her side.

Magda loomed above them with cruel satisfaction.

Over the witch's shoulder, Mup saw Crow's head thrust through the bars of his cage, goggle-eyed with concern, trying to get a look at her.

She waved a clumsy hand: I'm OK.

Magda slapped her face.

Emberly roared in outrage, and Magda zapped him with lightning.

Her hair and clothes seethed the air around her, her teeth were bared, and Mup thought, *She's gone mad!* Magda grabbed Mup's jaw. Her fingers squeezed hard into Mup's cheeks as she dragged Mup close. Her face was dreadful – *dreadful* – so sleepless and chalky and wasted.

Look at her, thought Mup. *So angry and alone. The only way to make herself feel better is to beat people up.*

"You think you're so great," hissed Magda. "With your sneaking around and your *talking to the queen.* Well, you don't *know* the queen. Whatever she told you, whatever she *offered you* is nothing but a game. I've seen it all before. It's her way of testing you – for pride and arrogance, for rebelliousness. She'll offer you the world and she'll snatch it away again until your head spins. In the end you won't know if she loves you or hates you, and you'll do anything – *anything* – to win her trust." She pulled Mup closer, her black eyes swallowing the world. "I've proved myself to her many times over the years. I've given her everything I ever had. You are not better than me."

When Mup didn't reply, Magda flung her away.

She snarled down at Doctor Emberly. "Fix the boy. I want him fit for purpose by sunrise."

She strode out onto the porch, slamming the door behind her. In the window, Mup saw her hesitate. The creature was staring at her, and something in his expression seemed to offend Magda's pride. "How dare you look at me like that?" she cried. "A hulking shambles like you. A hapless memory! How dare you judge me? Turn your face away."

The creature just kept staring. With a roar, Magda lifted her hand, ready to strike him.

Appalled, Mup scrambled to her feet. "Don't touch Crow's dad!"

But Magda never landed the blow. Instead, she allowed her hand to drift back to her side. She dropped her eyes from the creature's steady gaze. "I never loved you anyway," she muttered. "So you have nothing to fear from my touch." As if she didn't believe her own words, the witch thrust her hands into her sleeves and moved to the opposite side of the porch. "Drive," she said.

The vardo jolted to life as the creature slapped the reins.

"Let me out of this cage," hissed Crow, rattling the bars.

"Do take it easy, dear heart," gasped Emberly, pulling himself up by the edge of the table. "I... I shouldn't like to see you damaged any further than you already are."

"Lift me out of my body! NOW!"

"Lift you out of...?" The ghost looked aghast. "My dear boy, I don't know how to do that!"

"Whaaaat?"

Mup gaped at the doctor in horror. "You asked him to only temporarily step into his body!"

"Well, yes, I had assumed he'd just hop right out again."

"He doesn't know how! Neither of us do! The grey girl did it for us!"

"Get me out of here!" cawed Crow, battering the iron cage. "Get me out!"

"Calm down, Crow!"

"I'm so sorry, dear chap. I truly am."

"I can't believe I put myself back in this prison! And now my mam is going to offer me up to the queen like a bun on a plate."

The vardo rattled around them as it picked up speed. Mup paced to and fro, clutching her head.

"I need to get a message to Mam," she muttered. "I need to let her know where we are. If only I could touch the ground, I'm sure I'd be able to signal her, or leave a sign or something..." She pressed her face to the glass of the door. The mountains were looming fast, eating the sky at the horizon. "Do you recognize this landscape, Doctor Emberly? If you recognize it, you could zoom back to the palace and tell Dad and he..." She turned to the doctor, then hesitated at his ghastly expression. "You don't look well, Doctor Emberly."

"I don't feel well." The ghost slumped onto the chair. His face turned a very strange colour. "It feels like someone is using me as a stepladder, to be honest."

"Pardon?"

"As if a million geese were walking on my grave."

"What?"

The doctor clutched his ghostly chest. "Oh, my," he said. "That's rather an awful sensation... Is it possible, do you think, for one to unravel like a ball of wool?" Mup went to help him, but before she could even so much as take the doctor's hand, his troubled face cleared. He gave the most delighted smile, and addressed himself to the far wall. "My dear girl," he cried. "It's you!"

Just as Mup thought the poor ghost had entirely lost his mind, Naomi stepped from the bookshelves. "Doctor," she whispered apologetically, "I hope I haven't caused you any discomfort..."

"You followed me," he beamed.

Naomi nodded tenderly at him. "As surely as if you'd laid a thread down to guide me through the labyrinth of the dead."

Mup ran to the witch and hugged her. Without hesitation, the witch hugged her back.

"How's the grey girl, Naomi?"

Naomi shook her head. "I do not know for certain. She seemed to revive somewhat when I laid her in the oubliette. But she insisted that I leave before I saw any proper sign of improvement to her condition. It was she who insisted I venture onto the pathways of the dead. She told me how to track you, Doctor, how to follow the thread of light that stretches between you and your —" Naomi blushed as if mentioning something embarrassing — "your bones..." she murmured.

Doctor Emberly's cheeks flushed a gentle pink.

The witch looked away with a flustered smile.

Goodness, thought Mup with a blast of understanding. *Naomi is in love with Doctor Emberly!*

Obviously Crow thought the same. "This is no time for *romance!*" he cawed. "We're hurtling to our doom!"

The doctor laughed, startled. "Romance? Between Miss Naomi and I? Ha ha. Why, not at all! Miss Naomi and I could never begin to ... it's entirely *impossible* that we..." He met Naomi's eyes. His smile fell away. Mup saw him realize the truth.

"Oh, my dear," whispered Doctor Emberly. "My dear... You must know I could never..."

"Of course not," whispered Naomi. "Never."

The vardo jolted. In the porch, Magda rose to her feet. The wind whipped her cloak and hair, darkening the small room with flickering storm light. Mountains filled the sky. The witch's face was set in determination as she looked up and up to their summit.

Naomi crept forward. "Magda," she breathed, half in hatred, mostly in fear.

To Mup's horror, Magda turned, as if hearing her name. The occupants of the tiny space recoiled. Magda's expression did not change, she just tilted her head, cat-like, as she scanned the interior through the multi-coloured panes of the window. Over her shoulder the mountains grew and grew, casting their shadow into the tiny home.

Magda opened the door. Wind blew back hair and clothes and feathers. China rattled, curtains blew. Magda's hair and cloak writhed in the doorway. Her face was filled with hope and triumph.

"Sister," she said to Naomi. "Our mother sent you to guide me."

Outside the whole world was stone, the steep, grey slopes of the mountain coming up to meet the little wagon. Dust rose in harsh clouds as the tornado horses lightly touched ground. Gravel flew from beneath the wooden wheels. The vardo rattled to a grating halt.

In the sudden silence, Magda stepped into the vardo. She seemed to recognize Naomi's face and her expression became less certain. "You are one of the nameless," she said. "Yes. I know you. You are the one who is always being punished. The one who after ten full years of service has not even earned a name."

"My name is Naomi."

Magda's eyes narrowed warily. "That is not a queen-given name."

"It is the only name I need," said Naomi, raising her chin.

Magda's expression went flat. "The queen didn't send you, did she?"

"No, madam, I am not here to aid you or your queen. I am here to aid my friends."

Magda laughed her horrible laugh. "Some aid you'll be, a witch too stupid to even earn a name. I remember well how useless you are — how you botch even the simplest of tasks."

Mup took Naomi's hand. Naomi looked down in surprise. She squeezed Mup's fingers in gratitude. "Even the simplest of the queen's tasks are too cruel to fulfil," She said.

"I knew it," snarled Magda. "I've told the queen time

166

and time again that you were failing on purpose. I should have drowned you after your first year with us – you and your *flowers*, you and your *bumblebees*. But, *no*, the queen insists there is something useful in you. Chance after chance she's given you, and you've wasted them all."

Naomi clenched down tight on Mup's hand. For the first time in Mup's hearing, the young witch raised her voice in anger. "I should have run away from the queen the first chance I got! I should have used the power I was born with to—" She cut herself off with a gasp.

"To what?" Lightning grew in Magda's fists. "To *what*? Kill her? I'd like to have seen you try. I'll kill you now for even thinking it."

"MADAM, YOU WILL NOT!" Emberly stepped between them, his hands ablaze.

Mup leapt to join him, her hands raised and hissing sparks.

Crow threw back his head, opened his mouth, and sang a note so powerful it pushed Magda's hair back from her face. This seemed to frighten Magda, but even more than fear, she seemed confused.

"What are you doing?" she asked Mup. "That creature is not one of you. Why would you…?"

"Leave Naomi alone, Magda."

"But what *use* is she to you? She will not even summon

a flame to ignite a candle! With all the potential she was born with she chooses to hide behind you like a meaningless—"

"LEAVE HER ALONE!" roared Mup. "Don't you understand? Naomi doesn't have to be useful – especially not the kind of useful *you* want her to be! We love her because she's kind. We love her because she's *brave*. We love her because she's trying to save this world from the mess you made of it. *She's better than you in every way!*"

"Stop," whispered Naomi, covering her face. "Oh, stop. I don't deserve it..."

Magda allowed her arms to fall to her side. She looked from one to the other of the small group of defiant friends. "You are my prisoners," she said. "You..."

"No, madam," interrupted Emberly coldly. "No, we are not."

Something seemed to break in Magda at that, the last of her certainty drained away.

Mup almost, *almost*, felt sorry for her. *You have nothing,* she thought. *Nothing but violence and fear. Even Crow in his iron cage is freer than you.*

Magda stumbled for the porch. The creature, who had been peering in at the door, carefully drew aside as she passed him by. Magda leapt to the ground in a puff of dust, ran a little way up the narrow path and shrieked to the surrounding cliffs. "Majesty! Majesty, HEAR ME!"

Mup followed her outside. The air was breathlessly still and hot. Its silence seemed to eat Magda's shout. The witch stood pleading up at the dour mountain-face. "Please, Majesty. Please. Allow me home."

Warily, without taking her eyes from Magda, Mup climbed from the porch, crouched and pressed her hand to the gritty rocks. *Show me*, she thought.

A path crackled out from beneath her palm, sure and clean.

Down, down, down the hard face of the mountain, it went.

Out onto the flat grasslands.

Away, away, across miles of land so hot, and so dusty that Mup grew dizzy with thirst. The distance was alarming. *Just how far are we from home?* she thought.

Then... Oh, blessed coolness. Oh, sweet, soothing green.

Water. Life. The richness of earth softened by rain.

The relief was almost stunning.

Hope swelled large in Mup's heart as she realized where the path had taken her. It was the castle! The fields surrounding it were velvety with new grass. The forest was alive with unfurling buds. Glistening water cooled the thirsty rocks of the riverbed.

Inside, the castle was alive with many different kinds of people, all of them singing and dancing; all of them working together with innumerable magics to heal the damage Mup's grandmother had done. "They're fixing it," whispered Mup. "They're winning." The green was spreading out from the castle. Soon it would hop from village to village, from town to town as even more people joined their magics to the brew.

As quickly as it had been broken, the world was being healed.

Combined magic at its very strongest.

Mup glanced at Magda, still standing with her back to everyone. *You've lost*, she thought. *You and your queen.* She shook tears of happiness from her face, squeezed her eyes shut, and forced her will out through the network of paths of which she was the centre. She was searching for the cloud of raven guards who were out there somewhere, searching for the fierce woman she knew was leading them. *MAM!* she thought. *MAM! I'M HERE. CAN YOU HEAR ME?*

There was a jolt, a minute shock in the network, that told Mup she'd made contact. Mup pushed her will out more strongly, urgently projecting her thoughts, terrified that the connection might break before she got her message through. *MAM! WE'RE HERE WITH MAGDA. ME,*

CROW, DOCTOR EMBERLY, NAOMI. I'M NOT SURE EXACTLY WHERE WE ARE, BUT THE QUEEN IS CLOSE BY. SHE—

Suddenly all communication with the outside world stopped. Mup felt the pathways shudder beneath her palm. Then the whole powerful web sucked back into her hand with explosive force. For a moment Mup felt like her arm would explode. She screamed in fear and pain.

Then – *bam!* – the pressure released itself into one single pathway. The path shot away from Mup – a bleak, lonely road burrowing its way up the side of the mountain as if commanded by an unstoppable will.

A familiar, cruel voice spoke in her head. *Granddaughter. Come to me.*

Mup staggered to her feet, her arm numb from shoulder to fingertip. Emberly and Naomi had run onto the porch, drawn by her scream. The creature squeezed his way out behind them, carrying Crow. Magda turned to look.

Mup stared upwards at a darkness only she could see, roiling and seething at the top of the road.

"Grandma," she whispered. "Grandma is calling me."

Love

"What do you mean, the queen is calling you?" asked Magda, trudging behind as the group of friends made their way up the rocky incline.

Mup, a little way ahead of everyone and fixated on the darkness above, didn't reply.

Magda roared. "Answer me, you brat!"

Mup glanced back at her. No one else did. Emberly and Naomi continued to tramp forward, their eyes scanning the mountain for some hint of what it was Mup could see. Crow's creature clumped along behind them, carrying Crow's cage like a lantern held high.

Magda glared past them all to Mup. "Answer me," she demanded. "What do you mean, the queen is calling you?"

"She's told me where to find her," Mup said. "She's bringing me up there."

She pointed to the dark cloud that seethed at the top of the road.

Magda once again scanned the mountainside. It was obvious the witch wanted to see what Mup saw. It was equally obvious that she could not. "Why hasn't she shown *me*? Why can't I see her?"

In his cage Crow chuckled. "Maybe you're just no use to her any more, Mam."

This seemed to hit Magda like a blow. She stopped walking and just watched as the others trudged away. Mup kept glancing back at her for a while, but then she turned all her attention to the darkness that lay ahead.

The cloud filled a narrow gorge, dark tendrils of it twisting and grasping the air. Mup put her arm out to stop her unsuspecting friends from walking straight into it. They were right on the edge of the queen's domain.

"Oh, I feel it," muttered Emberly. "She's very close, isn't she?"

Mup stepped forward. She tentatively touched the cloud. It fizzed and buzzed against her fingers – an entirely unpleasant feeling. Mup pushed her arm into it.

Naomi gasped. "Your arm! It has disappeared!"

Mup looked back at her. "No matter what happens in here," she said, "I want you to just look and listen.

I think I know what Grandma wants. You're not to get annoyed when I promise to give it to her. All right?" The ghosts hesitated, then nodded. Mup met Crow's eyes. "All right?" she asked again.

Crow nodded grimly.

"I trust you, girl who is my friend,
You'll make things work out in the end."

Mup reached out her free hand. Naomi took it. Emberly took Naomi's other hand. The confused creature, after a little prompting, took Emberly's. Mup pushed onwards, leading her chain of friends into the cloud.

The air was thick and hissing as she forced her way ahead. It went against Mup's breath. Looking back, she could see the strain on Emberly and Naomi's faces as they followed her. Last to enter, the creature ducked his head like a frightened dog, and began to push through. He held Crow's cage against his chest. Crow's eyes were bright above the protective circle of the creature's dark arm.

Behind them all, Mup could see the slope leading away to the vardo, and Magda standing a little way down it, her eyes wide with astonishment. Everything was dim and fuzzy, like looking through an electric fog.

What do we look like from out there? wondered Mup. She recalled Naomi shouting, "Your arm! It has disappeared." Perhaps, from where Magda stood, they were all vanishing one after another. A chain of friends being eaten by thin air.

Magda stood there, gaping at them. Just as it seemed she would stand there all day, she snapped out of her astonishment. She shot forward. She made to grab the creature, who was still pushing himself into the magic barrier. But before she could touch him, he was engulfed.

Magda swiped at empty air, her eyes frantically searching.

She can't see us, thought Mup.

Magda stretched her mouth in a roar.

Mup saw the witch claw, then batter at the barrier, trying to force her way in. But she might as well have been hammering iron. She could not get past.

Then the air was clear again, and Mup had to turn her attention ahead, because she had broken through to her grandmother's domain.

Mup and her friends stepped from the magic barrier. Quietness hit them like a slap. The scuff of their feet on the dusty path seemed intolerably loud. The snap of cloth was the only other sound: the dark cloaks of one hundred raggedy witches fluttering with a life of their own.

Her grandmother had magicked herself a throne of marble. It stood at the top of the short slope, cold and

175

angular, just like the elderly woman who sat upon it. Her witches stood around her, their pale faces and dark eyes expressionless. They looked so sure of themselves. And why wouldn't they? One hundred witches, trained in the strongest magics, against two gentle ghosts, a none-too-bright creature, a bird in a cage, and a small girl in her pyjamas.

Appearances can be deceiving, though, thought Mup.

One note from Crow's mouth, and these smug, upright creatures would topple like bowling pins. One note from him and her grandmother would disperse like ash. It was over for them now. Mup was certain of this. She thought maybe Grandma was certain of it too.

Why else would she have offered to work with Mam, except to save her own skin?

The queen's pale blue eyes bore into Mup's as the little group of friends approached through the ranks of watchful witches. *What do they do here all day?* wondered Mup. *Just stand around?*

There was no furniture but the queen's cold white throne, no shelter but the grey stone walls rising on all sides.

The friends came to stand before the queen, who sat like a pale, amused spider, looking down at them from her elevated height.

Mup glanced nervously back at the narrow entrance that was the only way out of this gully. There was nothing to be seen there, except the swarming cloud of the queen's barrier. What was Magda up to, behind its dull facade?

As if sensing her thoughts, the queen gestured with her hand. Suddenly the cloud became transparent. Mup could once more see the steep path leading down to the vardo. She could see Magda, pacing to and fro. Magda slammed to a halt. It would seem she could see them now too. She ran forward and pressed her hands to the shimmering barrier, her eyes fixed hopefully on the queen.

The queen chuckled. "My wayward daughter."

"She still thinks you'll let her come back," said Mup.

"Why would I do that?"

"She gave her whole life to you. She betrayed her friends and murdered her husband and abandoned her son for you. Doesn't that mean anything?"

The queen huffed. "People are only of use as long as they remain loyal. She walked away from me in the heat of battle. She's nothing to me now."

Obviously capable of hearing these words, Magda shook her head in genuine distress. She battered the barrier like a child begging to come home. She was a terrible person, just terrible. But Mup couldn't help feeling sorry for her.

"Was it you who cursed her, Grandma?"

"Cursed her? Oh, you mean the ash thing. No. The stupid woman did that to herself."

Magda's face fell. She stepped back. She stared at her hands in horror.

The queen chuckled again. "You always were a sentimental fool, Magda. Could never truly let go of anything." She leaned to whisper to Mup. "She got everything she ever wanted. Then allowed her own remorse to steal it from her."

"Are you telling me all those things turned to ash because ... because Magda knew she didn't deserve them?"

"Damned fool."

Mup gazed down at the devastated witch. She thought of Magda's lovely house bursting into ash, all her pretty flowers, her affectionate cat. She thought of all the innocent trees and bushes and animals since then that had dispersed at Magda's touch. *She's the one who did wrong,* thought Mup. *She's the one who should be punished. But it's innocent creatures who paid the price for her guilt.* How like Magda.

"A guilty heart punishes itself," mused the queen.

"No fear of that ever happening *you*," cawed Crow.

"There's not a sorry bone in your body."

The queen turned her gaze to him. She rose creakily to her feet.

Magda bleakly lifted her eyes from her cursed hands, and watched the queen peer at Crow. The half-formed creature that had been Crow's dad frowned and grumbled. He huddled Crow's cage closer to his chest. Crow just glared through the bars, the silk bandages bright against his feathers.

"You're a little the worse for wear, aren't you, dear?" said the queen. "Did your mother do that to you?" She tutted. "Imagine damaging such a useful instrument. How did I ever tolerate her incompetence?" She ran her wizened fingers across the bars of Crow's cage. Crow snarled. The queen smiled. "I could make you invincible," she murmured. "A fierce little thing like you. You could rule half the world." Without waiting for Crow's answer, she pressed a finger to the cage. It disappeared in a gasp of mist, and Crow, a skinny boy with tangled hair and a bandaged arm, tumbled to the ground.

Emberly and Naomi leapt to catch him.

The queen tilted her head, as if seeing Naomi for the first time. "I know you," she said.

Her witches drew closer, peering curiously over the queen's shoulder. Naomi took a step back, obviously terrified. "Ah, yes," the witches hissed. "She is nameless. A tolerated one... A Useless."

The queen narrowed her eyes. She crooked her finger and Naomi shot across the space between them, brought closer against her own will.

Naomi shivered as the queen peered keenly into her face.

"By grace," breathed the queen. "You still have not used your powers." She shook her head. "Are you ever going to live up to your potential and make yourself useful?"

Naomi's fear seemed finally to leave her. She jutted her chin and looked the queen in the eye.

The queen sneered. "Such misplaced steel. No wonder you died."

She flicked her hand dismissively. Naomi spun backwards as if slapped. Emberly caught her and steadied her, and glared across her shoulder at the queen.

"And who are you?" asked the queen coolly.

Emberly's eyes flared. "I was briefly the castle doctor, madam. You did not approve of me. And so you had me tortured and killed."

The queen lifted an eyebrow. "Well, don't flatter yourself that I recall it. It was many a decade ago, judging by the outdated frivolity of your clothes."

"I do not flatter myself, madam. I am only one of many thousands murdered at your command."

The queen grinned like a cat. "Yes, well, that's the way of it, isn't it? Decades later, I remain the most important moment of your existence. While to me, you are not even a memory. Just a momentary annoyance, which I swept aside and forgot."

She snapped her attention to Mup. "I hope you're paying attention to all this."

"Oh, I am," said Mup quietly.

"Good. Learn the lessons of these fools. See what has become of them from wasting their time, talents or allegiances." She sat again on her cold throne. She fixed her icy stare on her granddaughter. "They came and went. Whereas I remain. Do not repeat their mistakes."

"Believe me," said Mup. "I won't."

"Do not allow your mother to repeat their mistakes."

Mup blinked.

The queen watched her carefully. "Your mother needs help," she said. "She's very strong and admirably fierce. But she cannot handle these continuing crises without me."

How dare you offer your help? thought Mup. *You murdered people. You tortured people. You stole their magic.* She didn't say any of this. Instead, Mup said, "You kidnapped my dad. You put me in jail. You tried to kill Mam when she rescued us. Why would I trust you?"

Grandma nodded. "It is true. I have said and done some harsh things to you. But that was before I knew your true mettle, child. Before I realized what a worthy heir you would make."

The witches all snapped their eyes to Mup.

Mup frowned in surprise. *Heir?*

The queen leaned forward. "Your mother is an excellent weapon, dear. But she's not like us. She's not clever and tricksy and wise. She is blunt force and brutality. She knocks down walls. You and me, though?" The queen leaned closer. "You and me? We build empires. We gather followers. We *rule*. Together, who knows what marvellous things we could achieve."

"Like end this drought?" asked Mup.

The queen sat back, pretending to frown. "Well," she sighed. "That might be difficult. I've never been terribly skilled at weather magic. But together —" she spread her hands, looked slyly under her lashes — "we might perform miracles."

You must think I'm some kind of eejit, Grandma, thought Mup. *I know you're causing this drought. Just like you caused the snow that came before it. And I know that you know that I know it!*

But maybe that was how queens worked. Maybe they

were always causing trouble, then offering to fix it – for a small fee, of course. Maybe it didn't matter to them that you knew what game they were playing, as long as you played along, as long as they got what they wanted in the end.

Once again, Mup was very glad that her mother never wanted to be Queen.

All business now, her grandmother straightened. She frowned with theatrical concern. "Your mother," she said, "might be a problem. Like I said, she doesn't seem to think as clearly as you. She allows emotions to cloud her better judgement. She may not be too happy to welcome me to her side."

"That's true, Your Majesty. But just between you and me, I think Mam could use your help."

The queen's eyebrow lifted. "Could she?"

"She's having a hard time coping with all these changes in the weather."

"Is she?"

"And the people are really starting to annoy her. The way they won't do what they're told."

"Are they?"

"Yes. Also, Mam does stupid things. She keeps saying she doesn't want to be Queen, for example."

"So I've heard."

"And she wastes a lot of time playing and eating and doing stupid stuff like that."

"I've heard that too."

"I think she could do with some tips on how to rule properly. Perhaps we could sneak you into the palace while Mam's away. Fix things before she returns. Explain to her that you rescued me from Magda. She might be so pleased that she'd stop fighting with you. Or something like that."

The queen's smile grew snakelike. "Or something like that indeed," she said. She raised an eyebrow at her witches. It was obvious she couldn't believe her luck. Mup could guess what was on the queen's mind. Safe passage through the kingdom with the heir's child hostage in the midst of her witches? Safe passage all the way into the sparsely guarded palace? Who knew what could be done with this opportunity. Who knew what havoc could be wreaked before Mam's return.

Mup's stomach tightened with disgust at the oily satisfaction on her grandmother's face. "You know what, Grandma?" she said. "I think you make a great queen."

"My dear child! What a lovely thing to say."

"I knew you'd think so."

The queen climbed down from her throne, spun Mup on her heel and began herding her down the path.

"Shall we head back right now, dear? By the time we get to the castle, I bet you and I will have already figured out how to fix the drought."

She was suddenly moving very fast for such an old lady. Mup could hardly keep her feet as the dry, hard hand propelled her forward. She glanced quickly back. Crow was limping scowlingly along beside his creature, hemmed in by expressionless witches. Emberly and Naomi were fleeting glimmers among the black.

Mup's mind was churning.

What if Mam can't handle the queen?

What if the queen can't handle the weather?

What if Crow can't handle his temper?

These thoughts were what was distracting Mup as her grandmother swept a hand to dispersed the magic barrier. The little vardo glowed like a jewel in the dull grey landscape. Mup kept her eyes on it, a hard frown hurting her forehead, her plans swinging this way and that. The witches were a dark tide flowing around her. Grandma's hand was firm between her shoulder blades.

Mup imagined herself and her friends inside the bright little wagon, flying over the scarred land. Would Grandma travel inside with them? Would her witches cloud the sky outside - their black cloaks darkening the air, their shadows passing over field and town?

How frightened people would be to see them again.

The queen was moving like a young woman now. No longer stiff, she strode intently forward, her thoughts fixed on some complicated future. She was so strong. She was so confident. It was easy to understand how everyone had done her bidding for so long. With a little flare of panic, Mup thought, *Maybe she's not beaten at all.*

She cast another anxious glance back at Crow. His glare was anger-black.

Maybe Crow should sing, she thought. Just one note would end it all. The witches would be gone. Grandma would be gone. Everyone would be safe.

Mup shook her head. No! she told herself. *Don't take the easy way out.*

Yes, Crow could destroy the queen if he wanted.

Yes, he could sing the flesh from her bones.

It would be a brave act. The act of a hero.

Except … the people of Witches Borough didn't need a hero. They were already their own heroes: all those small voices, all those little strengths that had joined together and stood up to the witches. They deserved the chance to tell the queen to her face that she had lost. They deserved the chance to tell those gathered around her that they would never again be tolerated. They deserved to always look back at this time in history and know that they'd done this. *Together.* Not in service of a brutal tyrant, but in order to protect each other, and their hopes for a lovely world where everyone could laugh and play, and live side by side in one glorious, jumbled, caring community of difference and respect.

Be patient, Crow, thought Mup. *Be patient.*

She tried to pour this into her expression. Tried make Crow understand how important this was: for him, for other people, for the future. Crow's frown softened. Whatever he saw in Mup's face, he nodded slowly in reply.

All right, Mup. All right. I can wait.

Mup smiled and he smiled grimly back.

Then Magda spoke.

She had been standing off to one side as the river of witches passed by, and had been ignored by everyone until that moment. She didn't shout, she didn't even sound angry, but her words cut above the scuff of feet and the flutter of cloth like a thin blade. "I loved you," she told the queen.

Silence descended as the raggedy witches turned to regard Magda.

The queen gave her a cruel, dismissive, horribly amused look. Her witches folded their hands. Sly pleasure filling their polished faces. They were looking forward to whatever the queen had in store for their former leader.

Somewhere in their ranks, Crow sighed impatiently.

Magda advanced, her eyes fixed in love and hatred on the queen. Her former brothers and sisters parted ranks to allow her through. Mup was mesmerized by the tragic look on Magda's face. By the smooth, confident way she approached her beloved queen. By the graceful billow of her black cloak as she opened her arms in a gesture both heartbroken and defiant.

Only Naomi guessed. Only she recognized the danger. Mup would be forever grateful to her for that … and for so much more. Mup and Emberly and Crow would have just stood there, watching, until it was too late. Except that Naomi turned to them and screamed.

"RUN!"

Emberly realized then. He spun and, in one loping movement, passed through four witches in his haste to get to Mup. The witches shrieked and toppled at the ghost's chilly passage through their bodies. Mup's vision went milky as he scooped her into his arms. She had only time to yell, "What's happening?" before Emberly was throwing her into the vardo.

Naomi snatched Crow and flew with him.

The creature seemed too stunned to run. He just

stood, gaping, as his wife, her face painted with tragedy and triumph, closed her arms around the queen.

"I loved you," whispered Magda into the queen's ear. "I gave you everything."

It took the queen so long to understand.

She'd been so sure of herself. Striding back into the life she'd temporarily lost, striding back to the palace and power and control. What could go wrong? Everyone needed her, including the heir who had stolen her throne. Soon everyone would bow to her again. Soon she would once again be queen of the world.

And so, when her outcast daughter came pleading through her merciless ranks of minions, why would the queen have worried? Why would she do anything except sneer, and wait with a half-pitying smile to deliver the final blow?

It was only as Magda's arms closed around her that realization widened the queen's blue eyes.

"I loved you," said Magda again, holding tight. "I loved you."

By the time the queen thought to struggle, she'd already started to dissolve.

She roared. Lightning ripped from her hands.

Magda held on, her arms clamped tight, as the queen's fire shook and scorched her.

They rose together into the air. The queen screamed and fought. Magda, eyes tightly closed, just held on. Ash and flame spiralled out. The raggedy witches stood like entranced children, their faces turned upwards as the two women spun faster and faster, blurring the air above them.

Mup gripped the porch rail, yelling "Run! Run!" to Naomi and Crow, who raced for the vardo.

"Dad!" yelled Crow. "Come on!"

The creature, finally hearing them, turned from his awed contemplation of the spinning queen. Realising his friends were leaving, he shoved the gaping witches aside and lumbered for the vardo.

He reached the porch as something burst within the frenzy overhead. There was no noise, just a silent shock, which slammed Mup's ear drums and made her duck and gasp. The creature pushed past her, dived into the driver's seat, slapped the reins and sent the vardo jerking into the sky.

Mup peered back through tears of pain at where the queen and Magda used to be. Ash blasted out as if from an explosion. The last things she saw, before ash filled the world, were the raggedy witches, their faces tilted upwards, their mouths open with amazement. The ash hit them. The witches had time to scream just once, before they were shredded to particles by the blinding storm.

"DRIVE!" screamed Mup.

The ash cloud blew outwards at tremendous speed. Ripping up rocks, scouring the mountainside, it filled Mup's vision with excoriating grey.

She was scooped into ghostly arms, and flung inside.

The door slammed just as the cloud hit the vardo.

Everything Dies

"DAD!" yelled Crow, elbowing out from Naomi's grip. "Dad, no!"

He and Mup ran to the door, but Emberly barred it with his luminous body.

"Doctor!" cried Mup. "Crow's dad is out there!"

For a moment Crow looked as though he would destroy the ghost where he stood. But then darkness filled the windows. The vardo came alive with hissing, shivery sound as a million harsh particles of ash scoured its wooden exterior.

Emberly moved aside. He knew they would not be foolish enough to go outside now. Crow and Mup crept to the windows and pressed their noses to the blue and yellow panes. There was nothing to be seen. Nothing but shifting, gritty darkness rasping the cheerful glass.

"Dad," whispered Crow.

"He must be still out there," said Mup. "Otherwise who's driving the vardo?"

With a bleak look, Naomi passed through the wooden door and out onto the porch.

She was briefly visible outside, then her light was swallowed by the crawling dark.

"Oh, my dear lady!" cried Emberly.

Crouching quickly, he pressed his hands to Mup's shoulders, looked hard into Crow's eyes. His gentle face was stretched tight with desperation. "Please," he said. "Please, my dear children. With all my remaining soul, I'm begging you. Whatever becomes of Naomi, the creature and I, do not come outside." Before they could answer, or even squeeze his hand, Emberly pushed through the door and out into the black.

Once again, Mup and Crow pressed their faces to the window. The hissing noise was all around them: the ash cloud rushing past. "I can't see anything," whispered Crow. "Not even a glimmer of light."

Mup spread her hands on the colourful panes. She could feel the movement of the ash beyond the glass – a harsh, sandpaper feeling against her palms She urged her will out into it, pushing the darkness back.

"It's getting lighter!" cried Crow. He thought deeply

for a moment, seeking something – some *rightness* of sound, maybe – then he sang.

Oh, such a gentle note, it was: a lullaby-note, soft, soft, out onto the scouring air. Mup saw the darkness brighten from pitch black to a gritty fog. In the fog, two person-shaped pillars of light wavered. "I can see them!" she cried.

Naomi and Emberly leaned side by side on the porch, their arms around each other's waists, their free hands clenched on the shoulders of Crow's creature.

Frowning and determined, the creature hunched over the reins, urging the horses on. The magnificent animals seemed not at all bothered by the ash. Why would they be? They were made of storm and cloud, nothing could hurt them. But they were not happy. Mup could tell by the lightning that flashed from their nostrils and sparked from their galloping hooves. It briefly illuminated their angry faces and frothy manes, before they were once again lost in gritty swirls of black.

The horses may not have been affected by the ash, but the creature certainly was. Despite the glowing protection of the ghosts, he was slowly dissolving. Clouds of grit rose from his shoulders and his hair to be snatched away on the raging wind. The storm was scouring him from the air.

Mup directed all her energy towards the creature. Crow sang his song directly to him. The bubble of brightness they had pushed out into the dark tightened around the creature's struggling form. Soon, all they could see was him, hunched valiantly over the reins, the ghosts' dim light flanking him in the ever-encroaching dark.

The storm howled on.

Rushing past. Scraping past. Bumping, hissing, seething.

Robbing the world of light and air.

It's never going to end, thought Mup in despair. *It's never, ever going to end.*

She and Crow began to sag with tiredness.

Still Mup pushed out and out. Still Crow sang.

They sent their strength out into the world. Out to their friends struggling in the dark.

Out and out and out.

And then...

Mup opened her weary eyes. OH, NO! Had she fallen asleep?

She was slumped against the windowsill. Her hands were cramped against the glass. Beside her, Crow leaned on the door frame. His eyes were closed. His head bowed. He was still singing, but only the faintest scratch of his voice remained.

Grey light painted the tumbled interior and Mup realized the dark had lifted.

She shook Crow's shoulder. "Crow," she whispered. "Look."

Outside, the air was misty and grey. Ash drifted downwards. The horses pulled the vardo sedately through it like picture-book horses through snow.

Mup and Crow stepped out into a wilderness of quiet. There was not a patch of colour left on the vardo. The storm had sanded every surface smooth of paint.

Emberly's sunken cheeks were luminous with tears as he scanned the veiled horizon. At his side, Naomi gazed bleakly ahead, her hand a glimmer on the creature's ash-coated shoulder.

Crow went to the creature. It did not lift its head in answer to his softly whispered, "Dad?"

Mup sank to her knees on the bare wooden floorboards. An endless vista of ash lay below her, nothing but grey fields and the dark skeletons of bushes as far as the eye could see.

"Everything is dead," she whispered. "They've killed it all."

An unfamiliar voice broke the eerie quiet.

Masculine, musical, kind, the voice said, "It's time for me to go."

It was the creature who had spoken. They all gazed sadly at it. It was still dissolving. Every gentle sway of the vardo, every soft gust of breeze, sent more of it drifting away into the foggy air.

"I know you're not really my dad," Crow said. "You're not really anything, I suppose. Just a collection of memories that somehow got bundled together and walked around for a bit. But…"

He reached his hand and very gently touched the creature. It had been gazing dully out across the landscape, the reins held loose in its lumpish paw, but at Crow's touch it straightened. Something like awareness creased its brow. The creature turned its head, and looked Crow in the eye. To Mup's astonishment, its diminishing substance drew together for one brief flare of clarity — and there was Crow's dad.

Toraí Drummaker, handsome and hawkish, clever and fierce, curved a tender smile at his son. He held out the reins. "You need to take these now, Crow."

Crow bit his bottom lip. Brightness shivered in his eyes. He took the reins from his father's hand, and Toraí was gone.

Crow gathered himself, sat into the driver's seat, and drove on.

They travelled onwards and onwards. The smothered grasslands gave way to forest, and they found themselves staring down into a bleak landscape of blackened, leafless trees.

"I hear ravens," whispered Mup.

It wasn't long before shapes appeared through the drifting veils of ash. Still a long way off, but growing rapidly closer, a great fluid cloud of ravens sped urgently across the treetops.

"Mam!" cried Mup, waving. "Mam!"

The flock changed shape, wheeled about, and headed their way. Soon the air around the vardo was filled with sawing caws and darkened by the flutter of wings. Ravens settled on the porch rail and the roof. They clattered and clucked and filled the surrounding sky.

"Better not poop on my woodwork," grumbled Crow.

A silver raven and a jet black raven swooped down into the porch.

"Mam," cried Mup again. "Fírinne!"

Mam landed and rose in one fluid movement, and

scooped her daughter into a fierce embrace. She smelled of ash and storm cloud and feathers. She hugged Mup tight, then looked her anxiously up and down. "You're all right?" she said. Mup nodded. "Crow?" asked Mam. "You're all right?"

Crow muttered under his breath. "If you call having my brand new paintwork sanded off 'all right'. If you call my vardo being crammed full of ravens 'all right'. Then I suppose, yes, I'm *all right*."

Mam pushed Mup's hair back off her face. Her hands came away fluffy with ash.

"Grandma's dead, Mam. Magda's dead, too. They killed each other."

Naomi whispered bleakly from her corner of the porch, "They took the world with them."

"There has to be something we can do, Mam," said Mup.

"Do you know how far this destruction has spread?" Emberly asked Mam.

Fírinne leaned against the porch rail, and grimly folded her arms. "We've been travelling through it for miles. It's expanding at a tremendous rate, smothering everything it touches."

Mup looked in horror at Crow. *Miles?* He swallowed hard, unable to hide his shock.

"They took the world," muttered Naomi again. "They took the world. And I let them..."

Emberly put his arm around his distraught friend. "What could you have done, my dear? We were all of us helpless in the face of their destructive selfishness."

"Let's go home," said Mam, softly. "Fírinne, lead the flock. I'll stay in the vardo with the kids."

They travelled quickly through ashy fog, across miles and miles of smothered landscape.

Mup wanted to fly down and press her hand to the ground, get some idea of just how far this deadening cloud had spread across their beautiful land. But Mam forbade her. So she spent the journey leaning over the porch rail, glaring keenly into the distance, looking for change.

After a while, Mam flew up to join Fírinne and the raven guard. They were nearing castle lands now. She wanted to be careful of threat. Naomi stood with Emberly's arm across her shoulders, her hands folded into her sleeves, her pale, young face ever more lost as the destruction rolled on and on.

"I should have done something," she said.

"There was nothing to be done, my dear."

"There *was*, Erasmus. Maybe not just now, but earlier. Much earlier, when I was..."

"When you were what?" said Mup. "When you were eight and your parents forced you to become a raggedy witch? When you were eleven and the queen was already punishing you for not obeying her orders? When you were—"

"Yes!" interrupted Naomi desperately. "Yes. All those times. Every time I had a chance I should have done something. Over and over again, I should have done something. Instead of hesitating and hesitating until it was already too late!"

Crow huffed. "All this from a ghost who won't so much as conjure a pot of tea on a cold winter's day."

Naomi pressed her hands hard into her eyes. She spun and stumbled through the wall, into the vardo and out of sight. Emberly gave Crow a disapproving grimace and floated after her.

Crow shrugged. "I'm not wrong," he said. "She talks about doing something but she still won't use the magic she was born with."

"Naomi died saving us from the little grey girl, Crow. She's not exactly done nothing."

"Maybe there wouldn't have been a little grey girl if Naomi had acted sooner."

"Well..." said Mup. "I like her."

"So do I!" insisted Crow. "I'm just saying, maybe

things would never have got this bad if people like her had done something sooner."

Mup couldn't argue with that. She leaned on the porch rail, and watched the ravens flying ahead of them in the misty ash. Crow went back to driving the vardo.

"I see green," he said.

Mup squinted. At first it was just unceasing greyness, but then, far off in the distance where the steady downfall of ash almost obscured the skeletal trees, Mup saw it too. A fleeting shred of colour through the foggy veil. As the distance lessened, Mup saw, clearer and clearer on the horizon, the bright green of healthy fields, the dance of green leaves on summer trees.

The raven guard cawed, and took on speed. Crow urged the horses to pick up the pace.

The fog thinned. The light brightened and they burst from the ash cloud. The ravens shed ash from their beating wings. The horses snorted ash from their nostrils and shook it from their manes. Ahead of them, the castle rose, strong and defiant, from green forest. Below them, graceful trees glowed under a benign sun.

Mup nearly cried at the beauty of it all. In her absence, the land had been completely healed. All those people in and around the castle with whom Marty had shared the Marshlander knowledge, all those people working together with their many small magics – they'd done it! They'd rescued the forest from her grandmother's terrible drought.

The castle battlements were filled with people, all of them looking back at the ash cloud.

The green banks of the river were lined with people, all staring in the same direction.

Mup launched herself from the porch and flew up to stand on the vardo's roof. Ash trailed behind them like a comet tail. They were already sixty yards or more from the ash cloud. It was shocking to look back and see just how impossibly huge it was. It filled the whole horizon, and it was still growing. Mup could see people running through the trees below her and along the forest paths. Some had nothing with them, some had bundles on their backs. They kept looking behind them and up at the sky. They were fleeing the cloud.

She leapt over the edge and flew alongside. Crow was thrashing the reins now, urging more speed. "Get back in the vardo!" he yelled. "These horses run much faster than you can ever fly!"

"I'm going down into the forest, Crow. I need to touch the ground!"

"Wait till we get into the castle!"

"No, I need to touch the *earth*. I want it to show me how big the cloud is!"

"How *big*? You can *see* how big it is!"

"I need to know how big it is *all around*, Crow. I need to know how fast it's growing!"

Crow shook his dusty head in exasperation.

"*Climb back in*," he sighed, "*and stand with me,*
I'll drive you down into the trees."

Mup clung to the outside of the vardo and Crow spiralled it downwards. The sun dazzled their eyes as they descended. A fresh breeze tugged their clothes. But by the time they neared the ground, the summer sky had hazed over. Greyness darkened the air. Ash drifted down to sprinkle the people's upturned faces.

The cloud was catching up.

Crow landed the vardo on the forest side of the castle river.

Mup leapt to the ground before they had even stopped moving.

She pressed her hand to the fresh green earth.

Show me, she thought.

Most Things Live

The pathways unfurled beneath Mup's hand. Tears forced their way from under her eyelids and cut clean pathways down her ashy cheeks as the horrible truth made itself known.

What lay out there was terrible.

Terrible.

The fresh green world was being eaten. All those brand new tender leaves, all that cheerful grass, all the joyful flowers and merry bumbling insects – the cloud was consuming them all. And it was huge. Huge and growing in every direction.

Oh, Grandma. Oh, Magda. What have you done?

A hand rested lightly on Mup's shoulder. She looked up into Crow's ash-filthied face.

"It's eating the world, Crow."

Emberly and Naomi drifted from the vardo. Ravens

spiralled down from the darkening sky. People came over the river, and emerged from the forest. They gathered together, ash falling on their heads and shoulders, and gazed down at the two children crouched on the green grass: the child and grandchild of those who had created this dreadful storm.

"We can't beat this," whispered Mup.

"We have to try," said Crow.

He was right. Of course he was right. Otherwise what was the point of being alive?

So Mup pressed her hand onto the suffering earth and closed her eyes. Crow pressed his hand onto her shoulder and opened his mouth. His voice filled her ears. A song of bravery and of strength. A song of never giving up. It travelled from him to her, and Mup pushed it out into the world.

Shadows fell across them. It was Mam and Fírinne. Dad and Marsinda ran up from a raft on the river. They pushed their way through the crowd to Mup's side. Ash dusted their hair and coated their desperate faces. They said nothing, just linked arms. Mam placed a hand on Crow's shoulder. Fírinne opened her mouth to sing, and Mup shut her eyes again, focusing everything on pushing their power out into the world.

One after another, Mup felt people join the chain. Little

flares of magic popped to life as people joined hands with their neighbour, or linked arms or hugged. She became the centre of a network of resistance as more and more people set their faces against the oncoming storm.

Mup pushed their magic out and out.

Still the ash rained down.

Voices rose in a heartbreaking chorus of defiance.

The trees shivered with power. The earth trembled with love.

Still the ash rained down.

At the edge of Mup's consciousness she felt the cloud inch closer. The earth was growing dull. She could feel silence loom. Desperately she channelled power out and out. She pushed it out with all her might. The relentless ash fell. It piled, soft and cold, on Mup's hands, on the back of her neck, on the top of her bowed head.

The air grew darker.

They weren't going to win. They weren't going to win. They were too small. It was too late. Mup gasped a sob.

Someone said her name.

Mup looked up. Her eyes were almost blinded with tears and narrowed with the strain of channelling so much power. Within her swimming vision, Naomi crouched. Glowing slightly in the deepening gloom, the witch's young face was expressionless as ever. Her black eyes calm. Doctor Emberly was by her side, his cheeks gleaming with ghostly tears. Around them the air was full of music and the hiss of falling ash. The people sang on, their faces tilted to the looming cloud.

Naomi rested her hand on Mup's. "I'm going to try and help," she said. "I hope I won't hurt you." She pressed down, and the world exploded in colour and light.

Magda had said, "You and your *flowers*, you and your *bumblebees*."

The queen had said, "Are you ever going to live up to your potential?"

Well, here was Naomi's potential. Here it was in all its glory. An explosion of butterflies seething the air. Seeds bursting upwards into towering trees. Roots burrowing slyly in the slumbering earth. Rivers wearing mountains to handfuls of stone. Naomi trembled with all of this power. So gentle and so unstoppable that, for a moment, Mup could do nothing with it.

Naomi opened her eyes. She pressed tenderly on Mup's hand, as if to get her attention. "Send me out, Pathfinder. Stitcher of Worlds, make use of me. Add my magic to your network of magic and together we might save the world."

Mup gritted her teeth. She clenched her jaw. She

squeezed her eyes tight and channelled Naomi's power out into the world.

It was like giving the earth back to itself. Like pushing and pushing at a locked door in a stuffy room until – SLAM – the door opens and the fresh air floods in. Power rippled from Mup's hands. Not with a boom. Not with a blast. But with a sigh.

Mup felt the earth *heave*.

She felt it shudder.

She felt it cast the ash from its hide like a horse shakes off dust.

And everything was right again. A million little blades of grass tickled their way up into the air. A million little baby leaves unfurled their shining heads. A thousand buzzing bees, a thousand dancing gnats, a multitude of earthworms, ants, butterflies and ladybirds, crawled and fluttered, crept and slithered beneath the gentle sun.

The gentlest summer rain began to fall.

Everyone turned their faces to its caressing touch, and smiled as it washed them clean.

Mup was hugged and kissed. Crow was snatched up and spun about.

The *clann* began to sing. The Marshlanders began a hideous, happy dance.

At one small lull in the celebrations, Mup looked across to see Emberly standing with his face to the rain, peaceful, but alone. She went to go to him, but Mam stopped her. "Let him be for just a minute," she said. "He needs a little time."

Naomi was never seen again.

Beneath the Gentle Willow

"There's nothing broken in the world that cannot be fixed, if people have the will to fix it. We need to work together, in all our differences. We need to walk together on all our many, varied paths. We need to listen in every language. We need to speak every truth. There will always be someone whispering that only they have the answer, that their way is the only right way. They will always be lying. Every path in life is distinct and valuable, every living being is equal and worthy of respect. You are precious. Your neighbours are precious. Your world is precious. That is the only truth. Let us live up to that."

The children's eyes slid longingly to the garden beyond the stained-glass windows and they shifted restlessly in their seats. Doctor Emberly sighed, and stopped talking. They weren't really listening to him. It was the last day of school. All his pupils really wanted was for their beloved teacher to set them free.

At the back of the class, Mup smiled. Her eyes met Crow's. He was leaning in the doorway, his arms crossed, waiting to say goodbye to the children. The last year and a bit had stretched his legs and sharpened his cheekbones and he was looking more like his dad every day. *He's getting tall*, thought Mup in surprise. It was the first time she'd noticed it. Perhaps because she and him were growing at the same speed.

Crow glowered at a particularly unruly child. *"Listen to teacher!"* he mouthed, and pointed the child's attention back towards Doctor Emberly.

The child straightened with military precision and turned to face the front.

Mup chuckled. Crow took these kids and their futures very seriously. Especially the small, frowning, lost ones. Especially the ones who didn't have many people to care for them. They flocked around him, these lost children, his little brood of grouchy chickens. Crow was determined to teach them that life could be good: that their future lay in their own hands. He taught them how to grow vegetables and sing. They called him "Mr Crow" and loved him beyond measure.

They're lucky to have him, thought Mup.

Crow came and leaned against the bookshelves by her side.

"Honestly," he muttered with feigned disapproval. *"These children's heads are full of boulders.*

I don't know why Erasmus bothers."

"They're listening," Mup assured him. "Even if they don't realize it. One day they'll remember everything he's said. And even if they don't..." She gazed across the restless, fidgeting youngsters to the gently exasperated ghost. Doctor Emberly's words were lovely, and Mup had no doubt the children would remember them. But they learned from him every day in other ways. His kindness taught them to be kind. His gentle strength taught them to be strong. His goodness taught them to be good. Just like Mam and Dad, just like Crow and Mup herself, Emberly taught these children just by being himself.

They'll never forget him, thought Mup. And in the autumn they'll come back, and he'll teach them even more about themselves, and about magic. And Fírinne will do the same, and Mam... And Dad will teach them how to do art and how to build things. And maybe there'll be more kids next year, and more the year after. And one day these kids will teach their own kids and things will just keep getting better, and stronger and...

"Everything's going to be all right," whispered Crow.

Whatever he had been thinking, his expression was now so wistful and hopeful that Mup almost hugged him. *Yes*, she thought. *Yes, Crow. Everything's going to be all right.*

"Well, I suppose I'd better let you all go," sighed Doctor Emberly, and the class exploded into delighted chaos. There came the screech of pushed-back chairs. Birds and butterflies and small fluttering bats took to the air as the joyful pupils transformed into their animal of choice. Some flew through the garden door. Some scurried, bolted or ran for the courtyard where their parents or companions would be waiting. Some stayed, shyly gathering around Doctor Emberly's desk.

Mup smiled at this particular group. They were the youngest pupils, the gentlest, and she was waiting for one in particular.

"I'll leave you to it," said Crow, as a group of scruffy children tugged impatiently at his sleeve.

"See you at dinner, Crow? Mam's cooking tonight."

"Do I ever miss dinner?"

Mup grinned. "No, Crow. You never do."

She watched him herd his companions up the corridor ahead of him.

One of the children said, "Can we help thee water thy plants before we go home, Mr Crow?"

"I suppose so."

"Can..." The child looked at the others. Nervous. "Can we visit during the summer and help?"

Crow faltered. He had reached the top of the steps, and he and his wild-haired brood were silhouetted against the sunshine. There were no guards at the door now, and the courtyard beyond was full of laughter and activity. The children's expressions were uncertain as they gazed up at Crow. Mup couldn't see his face. He pushed the hair back from a particularly filthy forehead. Ran his thumb over a scar on a child's eyebrow. "I guess I could use your help," he said.

Mup saw something in the children relax, a certain hard wariness left their faces. One of them took Crow's hand.

"I don't want any messing," growled Crow.

"No messing, Mr Crow."

"And you'd best help Mup's dad with his apple trees."

"Oh, yes, Mr Crow!"

They strolled out into the sunshine. Mup saw the flutter of shadows as they took to the air, heading up to Crow's camp and the ever-expanding garden he had there.

She turned back to the classroom. The shy children were mostly dispersed by now. She watched the remaining ones take their goodbyes until only one was left. Grislet bashfully reached up and pushed some small thing to the middle of Doctor Emberly's desk.

The doctor stooped over it, his eyes wide. "Is this for me?" he whispered.

Grislet nodded.

Doctor Emberly held the object up to the light. It was an ordinary pebble, brown and dull, and rounded from years at the bottom of a river. "Why, it's the most pleasing pebble I've ever seen. So smooth and cool. Thank you."

Grislet, utterly delighted, watched Doctor Emberly carefully place the small round object in among the twigs and feathers and leaves which the other pupils had presented him. His fingers lingered on the shelf. "I shall cherish these for ever," he whispered.

Mup crouched by Grislet's side. "Are you ready to go?"

Grislet nodded and took Mup's hand. Doctor Emberly accompanied them.

"Do you suppose Marty might join us next year?" asked Mup as they mounted the steps to the guardroom. "It seems such a waste for him to wait for you every day and never come in and learn."

"He *does* learn," said Grislet, skipping absentmindedly along at her side. "He hides on the windowsill and practises in the garden when none of you are looking."

Mup met Emberly's startled gaze. They immediately looked away from each other, afraid that if they acknowledged what the little girl had told them, she might realize that she'd betrayed her brother's secret.

"Ah, well," said Emberly. "I'm sure your dear brother will join us in his own time." He and Mup risked a fleeting grin, and said no more, but Mup's heart swelled in secret happiness. During the school year, witnessing Marty's gruff kindness and devotion to his sister, Mup had grown very fond of him. *He deserves to learn*, she thought.

They stepped out into evening sunshine and the sound of Dad's happy laughter. He and Fírinne were lowering the apple trees into their new homes. Over the past month, they'd removed numerous cobbles, making a series of large square flowerbeds all around the courtyard.

Fírinne slapped dirt from her hands, sighing, "I can't believe you're making a farmer of me."

Dad crouched in the dappled shade at the base of the new tree, and pressed good, rich earth against its roots. "Don't you think the place is better this way?" he asked.

Fírinne's face grew grave for a moment. She looked around the courtyard. Already the featureless walls were softened by the scent and shiver of blossoms, the buzzing of bees gentled the air. At the back of the yard, the names of the dead scrolled up and up. Fírinne regarded them through the hazy gold of evening.

Dad glanced up at her. "Are you all right?"

Fírinne smiled. "Better than I ever dreamed possible, Daniel."

Dad grinned, and held out his hand for the next sapling.

"Grislet! Grislet! Come here and help me dig another tree hole!" Tipper bounded over, his face and his paws all covered in dirt. Grislet ran to him, giggling. She offered her hand, and without hesitation, Tipper transformed into his little-boy form. The sunshine had baked him caramel-brown, and polished his golden curls as bright as his grin. "I bringed shovels," he said. "Because I knows you can't dig as good as me when I is a dog."

All business, the two friends set off together.

"Marty!" bellowed Grislet. "We need to stay because I have to dig a hole!"

Marty rose to his boy form near where Tipper had been "working". Mup smiled at the sight of him. He was always doing that — rising up from somewhere unobtrusive where he had been in his lizard form, watching over Grislet or, nowadays, Tipper. It wasn't a sly thing. More a shyness, Mup thought, a kind of uncertainty about himself. Mup made a game of trying to know where he'd be sometimes, but pathfinder or not, she could never tell where Marty might show up. She liked that.

Marty lifted his hand to her. She waved back.

Emberly began strolling towards the river. Mup followed.

"I do hope young Marty will come to school next year."

"He will."

The ghost quirked an elegant eyebrow. "You are a very persuasive young lady, my dear. I don't think your friends quite realize that about you."

Mup just grinned. They descended the boat steps.

At the river step, Mup crouched and let the water ripple, cool and sparkling, against her hand.

"What are you going to do now that school is over, dear?"

"I'm going to have fun, Doctor Emberly! Tipper and Dad and I are going camping with Crow. I'm going to teach Marty how to fly. Marsinda is going to teach me how to speak newt!"

"Delightful." The doctor was only half-listening. His attention was fixed on the giant willow tree which spread its graceful branches across the water on the far bank. It was so beautiful, the sun shimmering on its bright green leaves, the breeze whispering to the birds and small animals that nestled in the safety of its arms.

"Do you think it's really Naomi, Doctor Emberly?"

"Yes," he admitted gravely. "Yes, I do."

The tree had sprung up overnight, a week after the ash storm. Mup was quite certain that it had grown on the exact spot where Naomi had sacrificed herself. "I think it's her too," she whispered. "I think she let herself come back as something good and clean and beautiful. She gave everything she had and … and she felt like she'd earned a second chance."

"Perhaps," sighed Emberly. "I can't say for sure, because she never talks to me." He began to walk down the steps, slowly descending into the water.

"Doctor Emberly," said Mup.

He paused, waist-deep, and turned back to her.

"When Mam finishes her talks with the Northlanders, she and I are going to learn how to become fish."

"Oh, my dear!" said Emberly. "How touching! No one ever seems to want to be a fish."

"I don't like to think of you being lonely, Doctor Emberly. You spend so much time in the river."

The ghost gripped Mup's hand, and squeezed very gently. "I'm not at all lonely, my dear. I promise you. Even though Naomi doesn't talk to me. It's very lovely just to be near to her. Seeing the sun sparkle through the shelter of her branches, drifting in the cool water at her roots, one feels terribly peaceful. In any case, I'll be back in the autumn for the new students."

"Still … can we visit?"

"My lovely girl, my dear, *dear* princess, I would like that very much."

Doctor Emberly bowed his most ornate bow, kissed Mup's hand, and slipped backwards into the river. She saw him transform into a beautiful, luminous fish. She followed his progress under the water for a while, like a star weaving gracefully through the cool green, until he entered the shade of the willow tree. Then he seemed to dive deeper and was gone.

Mup took off her shoes and put her feet in the river and lay back on the warm stones. She could hear Tipper and Grislet in the courtyard, laughing. Dad and Fírinne's voices came and went as they moved about. Overhead, a shadow launched itself into the clear blue and Mup smiled as a familiar shape spiralled downwards. Crow's kids must have gone home.

Her friend swooped low, his wings skimming his own reflection, before fluttering up to land on the steps above her head. He chattered his beak. "Emberly's gone for the summer, then?"

Mup smiled and nodded, and closed her eyes against the sun.

Crow slipped down beside her and put his feet in the water. He leaned back on his elbows.

They lay there, side by side, for the rest of the evening, two friends at the beginning of a long hot summer, chatting and paddling their feet, waiting for Mam to come home.

Celine Kiernan is the critically acclaimed and multi-award-winning author of eight novels for young people. Her ghost story, *Into the Grey*, was the first book to receive both the CBI Book of the Year Award and the CBI Children's Choice Award. She is best known for The Moorehawke Trilogy, which has won multiple awards. It has been translated into nine languages. The Wild Magic Trilogy is Celine's first series for middle-grade readers. She lives in Ireland. You can find her online at celinekiernan.wordpress.com.

Jessica Courtney-Tickle is an illustrator and story-maker based in Cambridgeshire, UK. She graduated from Kingston University in July 2014, where she studied illustration and animation and found a specialism in children's books. Jessica loves working with colour, texture and lots and lots of characters. If she could choose anything at all to draw, it would be from nature or the theatre – or maybe both together! You can find Jessica online at jessicatickle.co.uk.